"Would It Be E...
To Say You W... Wonderful?"

Harrison asked, taking Paige's hands in his. "That the whole thing was…incredible, beyond my wildest dreams?"

"Mmm, yeah, but go ahead. I love a good lie, if it's told for the right reasons."

Her words pricked his conscience. "You know it's not a lie," he said, leaning down to kiss her.

"Thanks, Harrison," she said drowsily.

"For what?"

"That was the best bout of seasickness I ever had."

He tucked the covers around her the way he might for a precious child, then turned to leave. If he didn't walk away from her now, he never would.

Dear Reader,

Imagine that you're single and that you've been longing for a family all your life…but there aren't any husband prospects in sight. Then suddenly, a handsome, sexy rancher you don't know offers you a proposition: marry him. The catch—his four, lively children! Is it tempting? That's Kara Kirby's dilemma in this month's MAN OF THE MONTH, *The Wilde Bunch* by Barbara Boswell.

And a new mini-series, MEN OF THE BLACK WATCH, begins with *Heart of the Hunter* by BJ James. The "Black Watch" is a top-secret organization whose agents face danger every day, but now they face a different kind of danger—losing their hearts!

Also THE TANNER BROTHERS continue to delight us. Anne McAllister's *Cowboys Don't Quit* is Luke's story. And the HEART OF STONE series follows on with *Texas Temptation* by Barbara McCauley.

For a light romantic romp don't miss Karen Leabo's *Man Overboard*, and a single guy gets saddled with a baby in *The Rancher and the Redhead* by Suzannah Davis.

We hope you enjoy them all—we certainly do!

The Editors

Man Overboard
KAREN LEABO

SILHOUETTE *Desire*

*All the characters in this book have no existence outside the imagination
of the author, and have no relation whatsoever to anyone bearing the
same name or names. They are not even distantly inspired by any
individual known or unknown to the author, and all the incidents are pure
invention.*

*First published in Great Britain 1996
by Silhouette Books, Eton House, 18-24 Paradise Road,
Richmond, Surrey TW9 1SR*

© Karen Leabo 1995

*Silhouette, Silhouette Desire and Colophon are
Trade Marks of Harlequin Enterprises II B.V.*

ISBN 0 373 05946 9

22-9601

Made and printed in Great Britain

KAREN LEABO

credits one of her teachers with initially sparking her interest in creative writing. She was determined at an early age to have her work published. When she was still at school, she wrote a children's book and convinced a publisher to put it in print.

Karen was born and raised in Dallas. She has worked as a magazine art director, a freelance writer and a textbook editor, but now she keeps herself busy full-time writing about romance.

Other Silhouette Books by Karen Leabo

Silhouette Desire

Close Quarters
Lindy and the Law
Unearthly Delights
The Cop
Ben
Feathers and Lace
Twilight Man
Megan's Miracle
Beach Baby

One

___

Harrison Powell leaned against the railing of the *Caribbean Mermaid*'s Lido Deck, perusing the stream of passengers boarding below him. His gaze stopped on a tall, slender woman with a short cap of platinum blond hair. "There she is, in the red dress," he told the man standing beside him.

The other man, James Blair, peered at the woman through binoculars. He issued a low whistle. "That's her, looking sharp as ever. I can't believe she's fifty-eight years old. I thought she was more like forty-five."

"A face lift never hurts," Harrison said. His investigation into Aurora Cheevers's background had uncovered numerous interesting facts about her in addition to the cosmetic surgery. She'd been married and divorced four times; she was addicted to playing the Florida Lottery; and she had a twenty-seven-year-old daughter, Paige, who was even prettier than her mother, though in a much more subtle way.

The most fascinating fact about Aurora, however, was that her extravagant life-style far exceeded her income. Which lent credence to his theory that she was the *Caribbean Mermaid*'s jewel thief, the one he'd been hired to catch before any adverse publicity could get out.

"Would you stop staring at Aurora through those binoculars?" Harrison said, scowling at James, the ship's security director. A lot of pressure had been put on James to put an end to the daring thefts, which was why he'd hired Harrison.

"She's worth staring at, even if she is old enough to be my mother," James replied in a distracted tone. "Nice legs. You'll have some competition, I guarantee."

Harrison grimaced at the reminder of the plan he and James had agreed on. Aurora had a known penchant for younger men. Harrison intended to take advantage of that fact, playing the ardent suitor in order to stay close to her. If he couldn't catch her in the act, he intended to get inside her cabin and find conclusive evidence that she was the thief he sought.

James had wanted to simply wait for a theft to occur, then search Aurora's cabin. The ship's captain could authorize it. But the captain was adamant about protecting his passengers' privacy. He would not move against Aurora until he saw compelling evidence indicating she was the culprit. It was up to Harrison to provide that evidence.

The role of suitor wasn't one he looked forward to. His work usually involved behind-the-scenes investigation for the large security firm he worked for, not undercover jobs. But sometimes he didn't have a choice in which jobs he accepted. This was one of those times.

A younger woman standing next to Aurora caught Harrison's attention. He couldn't tell much from this distance, but... no, wait a minute. She did look familiar—petite and shapely, auburn hair that hung thick and rich past her shoulders, a generous mouth.

"Give me those binoculars," he said, nearly jerking James's head off as he made a grab for the glasses while the strap was still around the other man's neck. The moment he observed the magnified image of the woman, his suspicions were confirmed. "That's Aurora's daughter, Paige Stovall. What's she doing here? I thought Aurora always traveled alone."

"She does. I didn't know she had a daughter."

"That's why you hired me."

"Are you sure that's her?"

"I'm sure," Harrison answered grimly. He'd only seen her once, from a distance, during the two weeks he'd had Aurora under surveillance. But he'd seen enough of Paige to know she was the sort of woman who made his knees go weak, not to mention any good intentions he might have.

Green eyes, freckles and old-fashioned curves. The combination was lethal to his libido.

James reclaimed his binoculars. "She doesn't look much like her mother, but she's not bad, either. Damn. Do you think this will foul things up? Aurora might not want to risk stealing jewelry with her daughter around."

"I'll just have to keep the daughter conveniently out of the way, somehow."

"I could distract her."

The suggestive note in James's voice set Harrison's teeth on edge. He appraised the man anew. James was the sort a lot of women went for. He wasn't a large man, but he was blond and pretty-boy handsome, clean-cut without even the shadow of a beard. He might be able to turn Paige's head.

"No, James, forget it. Acting a role is a lot trickier than it sounds. I don't want either woman's suspicions to be even mildly aroused."

"Who says I'd be acting?" James countered, again peering toward the boarding passengers. "Blondes are more my style, but this chick is tolerable. And it's not suspicions I'd like to arouse."

Harrison closed his eyes and silently counted to ten. "James, this might be our only chance to catch Aurora Cheevers. Do not, I repeat, do not, screw this up."

He studied Paige once more. The wind molded her pistachio green skirt to her shapely legs and teased her auburn curls. Holding her hair away from her face with one hand, she laughed at something her mother said.

Harrison's mouth went dry. Tolerable? Paige was undeniably gorgeous, yet she carried an air of innocence about her that was endlessly appealing to Harrison. Too bad his job was to entrap her mother and send her to jail.

Paige Stovall hated every square inch of the *Caribbean Mermaid* before the ship had even cleared the Miami dock. She couldn't tolerate a lot of sun, she wasn't much good at shuffleboard, and the idea of Las Vegas-style shows made her long for her own bed and a good book.

And then there was the seasickness.

"Did you take your motion sickness pills?" Aurora asked.

"Yes, Mother."

"Paige," Aurora huffed, "don't call me that. I don't want anyone to know I'm old enough to have a twenty-seven-year-old daughter. For this week I'm not a day over forty-five, and you're my niece."

Paige could only shake her head as she hung her new clothes in the surprisingly roomy closet of their first-class suite. She had to admit their quarters were more luxurious than she would have guessed possible aboard a ship. They even had a small veranda.

Her mother's room was on the other side of a connecting door. She'd tried to get Aurora to share a single cabin, but Aurora had ruled that out immediately. What if one of them had a guest? she'd discreetly pointed out.

That's just what Paige was worried about. Aurora was definitely on the prowl—husband hunting again. Every time she went on a cruise, she came home married, or nearly so. Paige was determined her mother was not going to hook up with another loser.

Aurora eyed her daughter's simple green skirt and cotton print blouse, then pursed her lips disapprovingly. "You're not going to the cocktail party like that, are you?"

"What's wrong with this?" Paige asked defensively.

"Well, nothing, if you're teaching school. But this is a cruise. Liven up, girl! Put on one of those cute outfits I bought for you. First impressions are essential. You want to make an impact during the first of-

ficial cruise function, start carving out your territory."
As she spoke, she pawed through Paige's closet.

Paige wondered what Aurora meant by *carving out territory*.

"Now this—this is perfect," Aurora said, pulling from the closet a crisp, white shorts outfit trimmed in navy blue piping. "I have a little navy straw hat that'll go perfectly. Wait right here." She thrust the outfit at Paige and disappeared through the connecting door.

With a sigh, Paige began undressing. This was a familiar scene. Aurora was always trying to turn her daughter into a clothes horse, and it never worked out. With her short stature and curvy figure, Paige simply wasn't the high-fashion type. Whenever she took Aurora's advice, she ended up looking like an overdressed doll instead of a sophisticated woman. But Aurora simply refused to understand that Paige's personal style was quite different from her mother's.

Well, what did it matter? Maybe if Aurora spent the next seven days dressing Paige and telling her how to behave on a cruise, she would be too busy to meet and fall in love with some freeloading bum.

Aurora had a real talent for picking the most inappropriate men to marry. The only exception to that rule was Aurora's first husband, Paige's father. He was the one who'd convinced Paige to brave the hated cruise ship in order to keep her mother out of matrimonial trouble. Bobby Stovall had bailed Aurora out of more than one disastrous marriage and continued to support her financially, although his legal obligation to do so had ended long ago. He was still genuinely fond of her—but he'd made it clear that if she married again, he would cut her off for good.

Paige didn't want that. Aurora needed Bobby, although she would never admit it.

Fifteen minutes later, feeling rather foolish in the hat Aurora had insisted she wear, Paige walked with her mother onto the Lido Deck, where a lavish buffet of fresh fruit, cheese and crackers awaited them. A smiling waiter thrust a glass of champagne into Paige's hand. Since champagne always gave her a headache, she set the full glass on the first empty tray she saw.

"Come on, let's get in line for the food," Aurora said as she surveyed the milling crowd with a practiced eye. Then, under her breath, she added, "Gawd, is there anyone here under seventy?"

There did seem to be a preponderance of silver hair and canes among the *Caribbean Mermaid*'s passengers, but no shortage of male hormones, if the stares Aurora drew were any indication. Even in her clever new outfit, Paige felt like a plain brown duck next to her mother.

It had always been like that.

The two women found a table and sat down with their plates of fresh fruit. Aurora nibbled at a melon wedge disinterestedly as she continued to eye the crowd. "Where are all the good-looking men?"

"What about that one over there?" Paige said, nodding toward a distinguished, sixtyish-looking man with a head of thick, silver hair and a healthy tan. He looked pretty respectable.

"Oh, that's Doc Waller," Aurora said with a dismissive wave of her hand. "He's a widower. I've met him on several cruises. He's quite a nice gentleman, but...too old for me. They're all too old. I hope this cruise doesn't turn out to be a total waste of—wait a minute!" She grew very still, and her sharp blue eyes stared intently at some point in the distance. "Would you look at that?" she whispered.

"What?" Paige asked, squinting in the same direction. Then she saw him, and she wondered how they'd missed him before. Standing a good head taller than most of the people around him, he possessed the sort of lean, hard good looks one might expect to see on a man driving a race car or climbing a mountain. His hair, a rich, dark brown with slight silvering at the temples, was longer than conservative fashion dictated, and the wind rippled it like a woman's fingers would. His impossibly wide shoulders stretched the confines of the cotton print shirt he wore, and his legs appeared too muscular, too powerful, for his tame, white twill shorts.

He was easily the best-looking man Paige had seen in months. Years, maybe. Unfortunately, there was a comely dark-haired woman clinging to his arm.

He was talking to another man, one of comparable age—late thirties, Paige guessed—and nice looking, but not in the same league as the tall, dark-haired one.

"Not bad, eh?" Aurora commented from the side of her mouth. "And there are two of them."

"Mother! Aside from the fact that they're both young enough to be your—"

"Bite your tongue," Aurora whispered. "And stop calling me Mother."

"All right, Aurora. But you talk like those two men are a couple of ripe plums we can just pick from a tree. What makes you think either of them will have the slightest interest in us?"

"Instinct, my dear," Aurora purred. "And besides, I don't see much competition."

"You don't see the large-breasted brunette in the halter top, breathing into the taller man's ear?" Paige asked dryly.

"Oh, her. She's too young to hold his interest for long. Now, a man like that, he no doubt appreciates a woman with a little sophistication, one who's been around the block."

"How about one who's been around the world a couple of times?" Paige murmured.

"What?"

"Nothing. Oh, Lord, they're coming this way." Paige quickly pretended interest in her strawberries.

"Well, of course they're coming this way. I gave them my look."

"What look?"

"The one that says, 'You interest me.' Not too bold. Just a brief holding of eye contact, between one and two seconds. Oh, nuts, that bosomy brunette waylaid them again."

Paige looked up. Her gaze immediately caught and held with the dark-haired man's—one second, two seconds, three, four...

"Psst! Paige, that's long enough," Aurora hissed.

Paige reluctantly broke eye contact. "What?" she asked, feeling a little dazed. His eyes were dark brown, just like his hair. Even from this distance she could easily lose herself in those velvety brown depths.

"The look you're giving him is saying a lot more than you want it to, I'm afraid. Watch it."

"Watch what?"

Aurora threw up her hands. "How in the hell did I raise such an innocent daughter?"

"Just because I don't play games with my eyes doesn't mean I'm innocent," Paige pointed out. "Anyway, what's wrong with a little innocence?"

"It's no fun, that's what's wrong."

"Well, I may not be the most worldly woman, but at least I don't get married at the drop of a hat." The unfortunate words were out of Paige's mouth before she could stop them, and she immediately regretted her pettiness. For all her seeming worldly sophistication, Aurora really was the naive one. Despite her checkered past filled with less-than-honorable men, she still would believe anything a handsome man told her. She had never developed that hard edge of cynicism so common among women of her age and circumstances.

"I may be divorced four times, but I've fallen in love and married four times, too," Aurora said quietly. "And I wouldn't trade those experiences for anything. There is nothing more glorious than falling in love, even if you know it's not going to last. And you, my dear, are going to be a dried-up prune by the time you're thirty if you don't find yourself a man." She downed the last of her champagne in one gulp and banged her glass on the table so hard that Paige jumped.

"I'm sorry, Moth—I mean, Aurora. That was an ugly and hurtful thing I said, and I didn't mean it."

Aurora wiped her mouth delicately with her napkin. "And you're a long way from being a prune," she conceded gracefully. "If only you'd loosen up a little..."

"I'll try. I promise." And maybe she really would. That man with the brown eyes could certainly inspire her to try. Of course, that was probably just her neglected hormones talking. Her love life could definitely use some shoring up. It wasn't that she didn't want a man in her life. She just didn't seem to communicate well with the opposite sex, at least not on a romantic wavelength. Most men tended to treat her like someone's kid sister.

"Mind if we sit down?" a voice beside her asked.

Paige almost swallowed whole the strawberry she'd just popped into her mouth. He was here, Mr. Gorgeous, sans the brunette. He stared at her with those warm brown eyes, his gaze checking her out in a most unbrotherly way, roaming from the top of her head to her waist and back up, lingering on her full breasts. Her nipples tightened reflexively, and she could only hope they didn't show.

Her face grew warm as she struggled for something clever and sophisticated to say.

"Please, join us," Aurora said, easing over the awkward moment. "I just love meeting new people on these cruises. I'm Aurora Cheevers, and this is my niece, Paige Stovall."

Both men nodded and sat down, offering their names, as well. The tall one was Harrison Powell, a name that seemed to fit perfectly; the shorter, blond man was James something. Paige didn't like the way James looked at her, although his gaze certainly wasn't as bold as Harrison's had been.

"Is this your first cruise?" Aurora asked both men, but her eyes focused on Harrison. She tapped a cigarette out of a pack she'd pulled from her purse and inserted it into a holder. Harrison took her lighter and flicked it, cupping his hand around the flame to protect it from the wind.

Aurora touched his hand briefly to steady it, then smiled, a sly, cat's-in-the-cream smile Paige had seen a hundred times.

Inwardly Paige sighed. Her mother sure didn't waste much time.

"Actually, this is my first cruise," Harrison said. "And you?"

Aurora gave a throaty laugh. "Oh, my goodness, I've lost track of the number of cruises I've been on. I'm positively addicted to the Caribbean. But this is Paige's first, isn't it, dear?"

"Yes. Mmm-hmm." Brilliant. Her mind felt like it was on novocaine.

"And what about you, James?" Aurora asked. "I do believe you look familiar to me."

"I work for Mermaid Cruise Line, in administration," he said with a charming smile. "I'm usually holed up in the offices down in the bowels of the ship, and I don't often get to socialize with the passengers. My loss." He looked at Paige as he said this.

Oh, brother, she thought. This James obviously believed he was a real smooth operator. Well, he could just operate on someone else. She wasn't interested.

Now, Harrison was another story.

"What made you decide to come on a cruise?" Aurora asked Harrison.

"Actually, I'm thinking of investing in the Mermaid Line. But I never put my money into something without thoroughly investigating it first." He shrugged. "This is part of the investigation."

"And do you like what you see so far?" Aurora asked.

"Very much."

Aurora's and Harrison's gazes locked for a brief interlude. But not so brief that Paige didn't see what was going on. Her mother was in the process of making another conquest.

The realization hit Paige in the stomach. It shouldn't bother her, really. Men were always attracted to Aurora. Men fell in love with Aurora. They flocked around her in crowds, vying for her attention. She was so sweet and easy to be with, they said. Instinctively she knew just how to make them feel handsome and desirable and utterly masculine.

Paige had witnessed it dozens of times. Why, then, did it suddenly bother her so much? Was it because the object of Aurora's attention just happened to be the one man on this whole godforsaken ship that interested Paige?

Feelings Paige thought she had long ago dealt with rushed to the surface. The incident with Curtis Rittenour hadn't been Aurora's fault, she reminded herself. Aurora had just been her usual bubbly, charming self.

Curtis had been an older man—all of thirty-four to Paige's star-struck twenty-three—and a sophisticated, wealthy doctor. Paige had been convinced he was her destiny. The man had showered her with attention. He'd seemed very pleased when Paige had nervously invited him to travel to Ft. Lauderdale with her from Miami, where she was in graduate school, and meet her mother.

Poor Curtis. He hadn't even had a chance. The moment he'd set eyes on Aurora, he'd fallen in love with the swiftness of a diver leaping from the high board—although without the grace.

To her credit, Aurora had not encouraged him in any way. But Aurora didn't have to encourage. Smitten, Curtis had pursued her relentlessly to the point of buying her a diamond ring. Never mind that Aurora had made it clear she did not reciprocate his feelings. It had taken Bobby's intervention to get rid of the guy.

All that was ancient history, Paige reminded herself. But the remembered pain brought on by Curtis's betrayal still could give her a twinge now and then.

Like now. Only this was more than a twinge.

Harrison laughed at something Aurora said. It was a low, full-bodied laugh that skittered pleasurably up and down Paige's nerve endings, bringing goosebumps to her arms. His lips were full and sensual, his teeth even and white.

The man Aurora had identified as Doc Waller wandered up and joined their party. Within moments he was hanging on Aurora's every word. Even James, who earlier had been looking at Paige with something akin to interest, seemed to have forgotten her existence. She felt utterly invisible.

This was ridiculous, she told herself. There was no reason in the world she should begrudge her mother's enjoyment. If anything, she should be overjoyed that the object of Aurora's attentions appeared to be a wealthy and stable man, not some penniless fortune hunter.

Of course, appearances could be deceiving.

Paige stood abruptly. "I hope you'll all excuse me, but this afternoon sun is so strong, it's given me a headache. I think I'll go lie down for a while."

She tried to stand and make a graceful exit, but her purse got hung up on her chair. A gusty breeze nearly unseated her hat. The last thing she saw before she managed to disentangle herself and make her ungainly escape was Harrison, watching her, obviously amused.

Two

_____

Harrison turned his attention back to Aurora, but his thoughts were with Paige. What was troubling her? he wondered. He'd gotten the distinct impression that she wasn't ill so much as irritated.

Aurora's gaze was locked on the retreating form of her daughter. "Now I wonder what's eating her?" she asked with a worried frown, echoing Harrison's thoughts. "Maybe I should go check on her. She's prone to seasickness."

James stood up. "I'll see that she gets back to her cabin all right."

"And I've got plenty of seasick pills with me," Doc Waller added, starting to rise also.

"Oh, please, don't bother," Aurora argued amiably. "Besides, James, I have a million questions I want to ask you about running a big cruise ship like this one. It must be fascinating work. And you, Doc—

the last thing you need is to be taking care of sick people on your vacation. But maybe...'' She batted her eyelashes at Harrison. ''Would you mind, Harrison, seeing that my niece makes it safely back to her cabin? We're on the Marlin Deck.''

''Sure, I'd be happy to.'' Happier than he'd like to admit. He was supposed to be romancing Aurora, but that was a damned impossible task with her daughter sitting across the table. Now that Paige was out of the way he should lay it on thick. But all he could think about was running after her to find out what the problem was.

Well, Aurora had asked him to do it, he reasoned. And he wanted to please her, right?

''I'll be back.'' He gave her what he hoped was a charming smile as he stood and turned to make his escape.

Harrison had no trouble catching up to Paige. She had paused at the buffet table to sample some Brie cheese on a cracker.

''Must be some headache,'' he said from behind her.

She made a startled little noise and whirled around, her face turning pink. ''Oh, it's you. I thought maybe some cheese and crackers would help the headache,'' she said, crossing her arms defensively. ''Protein and carbohydrate to increase the blood sugar, you know. Besides, Aurora signed us up for the late dinner seating, and I haven't eaten all day except for those few strawberries.''

He remembered the strawberries. He'd hardly been able to keep his eyes off her as she'd delicately nibbled the juicy red morsels.

"In that case, try some of this Swiss cheese." He stabbed a small yellow cube with a toothpick and held the tidbit in front of her mouth.

After giving him a suspicious look, she reluctantly parted her moist lips and plucked the cheese cube from the toothpick, then chewed it thoughtfully. "Mmm, you're right, it is good," she conceded.

"How about some white cheddar on a wheat cracker?" He cut a generous slice of the thick, white cheese, set it on a cracker and handed it to her. He'd almost held it in front of her mouth again, just for the sensual pleasure of feeding her, but he figured that would be pushing his luck. While she munched on the treat, he popped a slice into his own mouth.

"Headache any better?" he asked.

"I guess I don't really have a headache," she admitted. "I just get annoyed watching Mo—Aurora flirt so shamelessly."

"Why does it annoy you? Flirtation is a dying art, and she's very good at it. Besides, it's fun. You ought to try it."

"No, thanks," Paige said with a haughty frown. "I'd rather be a bump on a log. I'm very good at that."

"I didn't mean to imply you were a bump. In fact, you don't resemble any part of a log."

She gave him an appraising look. "Are you flirting with me? Hedging your bets in case Aurora doesn't take your bait?"

He didn't answer. She'd caught him. But he couldn't help himself. Paige Stovall begged to be cajoled into a smile, and he wanted to be the one to do it.

He'd better cut it out, he decided, or he would alienate both women. A man who set his sights on a mother and daughter—or an aunt and her niece, as he was supposed to believe them to be—could only be labeled a jerk.

"Well, I suppose it's none of my business if you want to throw yourself at Aurora," Paige said. "But I should warn you, her flirtations are anything but innocent. She's been married four times."

Harrison was careful to show the appropriate degree of surprise. "Really?"

"And I'd be leery if I were you. She might have you selected as husband number five."

"I think you're exaggerating. We were just enjoying a conversation. But would it bother you terribly if she had set her sights on me?"

"Damn right, it would! She's old enough to be your... well, your much older sister."

"I don't see that age is so important. In fact, I'd guess the age difference between Aurora and me isn't as great as the one between me and you." Actually, he was about ten years older than Paige and more than twenty years Aurora's junior. But he wasn't supposed to know that.

"The age difference between us isn't the issue." She shrugged, though she didn't appear as unaffected as she pretended. "Think what you like. But I warn you, I won't let Aurora have her head turned by another handsome younger man, who has nothing in common—"

"You think I'm handsome?"

She blushed again. "What I think about you isn't important." She turned away, clearly dismissing him, and left the buffet table.

Harrison wasn't finished with this conversation. Paige's concerns about her mother fascinated him.

Had she come on this cruise solely to protect Aurora from male predators like the cad she thought him to be?

He followed Paige to the railing, where she paused to look out over the inky blue water. Taking up a position beside her, he said, "If you're trying to prevent your aunt from marrying another loser, you have nothing to fear from me. I find her charming, but I have no intention of marrying anyone, not in this century."

Paige tilted her head and looked at him skeptically through slitted green eyes. "So you'd rather use her and drop her? Oh, that's reassuring."

"What makes you so sure I intend to 'use her,' as you so delicately put it? Couldn't I just enjoy her company?"

"If that's all you're after, you would be an unusual man indeed, certainly for Aurora," Paige said. Her head was lowered, her face hidden from view by the wide brim of her ridiculous hat.

Wanting to see her face, and those incredible green eyes, he impulsively pulled the hat off her head. She looked up suddenly, surprise and confusion warring on her expressive face.

"Who gave you such a low opinion of men, Paige Stovall?" he asked. When she looked away, refusing to meet his gaze, he touched her chin and gently drew her face toward him again.

"I'm just a realist," she countered. "When a man approaches a woman, he has one of only two things on his mind."

"Is that so? Which do I have on my mind right now?"

She stared at him, her eyes wide with surprise, and for a moment he worried that she really could read the less-than-pure thoughts in his head.

"I don't know, and I don't really care," she finally answered, grabbing her hat from him and jamming it on her head. "Now, if you'll excuse me, I'm going back to my room."

"I'll walk with you," he said affably, despite the withering dismissal she'd just given him.

"That won't be necessary."

"But I promised Aurora I'd see you safely back to your cabin. She was worried about you. Umm, the elevators are this way," he added when Paige took a wrong turn.

"How do you already know so much about the ship?" she asked, accepting his company for the moment, the way someone accepts taxes and junk mail. "I thought this was your first cruise."

"The Mermaid people invited me aboard a day early, so I could observe the cruise preparations. It seems to be a very efficient operation."

"Then why do they need your money?" Paige asked as she and Harrison stepped aboard the elevator.

"Expansion takes capital. Mermaid wants to build a new ship. I'm looking for a way to shelter some of my income for the next couple of years." He hoped she didn't delve any deeper than that into his supposed background. His knowledge of the world of high finance was abstract at best.

Besides, he really hated lying, even if lying was a part of his job. Paige already had a less than sterling opinion of him. He didn't like giving her more fuel. In fact, he found himself wanting to convince her that there were honorable men on this earth, men who were after more than sex, money and power. He wanted to prove to her that he was just such a man, a man who could value a woman's intelligence as well as her body, one who enjoyed quiet walks in the moonlight as much as a night of mindless passion in bed.

But he could hardly prove that to her when it wasn't entirely true. When it came to Aurora, he might not have money or sex on his mind, but he did have an angle, a self-serving angle. And when Paige discovered he wanted to put her mother in jail, he wasn't likely to climb in her estimation.

When he and Paige arrived at the door to her cabin, she had to fish around in her handbag for the pass card. Harrison leaned one shoulder against the door frame and folded his arms.

"You could at least give me the benefit of the doubt," he said. "I might not be the ideal match for Aurora, but with me hanging around, she won't have time to take up with someone even worse than me. That is what you're worried about, right?"

Paige seemed to consider his words. "If you and Aurora want to spend time together, there's not much I can do about it. And I suppose she could do worse than to fall for some wealthy financier—if that's what you are. But just remember this—I'll be watching. And if I find out you're not who you say you are, I'll show no mercy." She shoved the magnetic card into the slot and jerked it out, then tried the door. It didn't open.

"You did it too fast," Harrison said.

"I know how to open a door," she said impatiently as she repeated the procedure. This time she got the flashing green light, opened the door, stepped inside and closed it again—firmly.

Harrison felt a pang of guilt, and he had to remind himself again that this was all part of his job. He was being paid to catch a jewel thief. But it seemed grossly unfair that the thief's innocent daughter would be hurt in the process.

On the other side of the thin door, Paige held her breath until she was sure Harrison was gone and then released a long, tension-filled sigh. The nerve of that man, hitting on two women at the same time.

Well, okay, Paige conceded, he hadn't really been hitting on her. But she'd had this vague but undeniable feeling that something had been going on between them, something sort of . . . sexual.

Or maybe she was imagining things. As Aurora so often and annoyingly pointed out, Paige was no expert when it came to men and their baffling ways. Maybe it was only wishful thinking on her part that a wealthy, good-looking man like Harrison ·Powell would take any interest in an ordinary hospital dietitian like her.

She threw the silly navy hat onto her bed, then followed it, sitting gingerly on the mattress and leaning her head against the wall. How was she going to keep Aurora from making a fool of herself over this guy? And did she really want to? Harrison had made a valid point when he'd said that, so long as he kept Aurora interested, she wouldn't have time to fall in love with an even worse prospect.

An insidious, nasty thought worked its way into Paige's consciousness. There was one way she might be able to keep Aurora and Harrison apart, and that was to throw herself at Harrison. For her it would be only a meaningless shipboard romance, and through her efforts she might just keep Aurora from walking down the aisle a fifth time. Despite Harrison's reassurances that he didn't have marriage on his mind, he might yet fall victim to Aurora's charisma.

Nice try, she told herself, attempting unsuccessfully to tamp down her bubbling self-disgust. If Harrison had the slightest interest in her—and that was a big *if*—it was inexcusable of her to even think of stealing the man her mother had her eye on. And if the very idea weren't laughable, such a despicable act was not the way to bolster her ego and assuage the five-year-old hurt of Curtis Rittenour's defection.

When Aurora finally returned from the cocktail party—half-looped, in Paige's estimation—she solicitously asked after Paige's headache. Paige resisted the urge to snap, since Aurora had done nothing wrong per se, and gave a noncommittal reply.

"You'll feel better once you eat some real food," Aurora soothed. "I heard there's shark on the menu tonight. James says they have a new French chef who's marvelous. He has his own TV show and everything."

"Mmm," Paige said, waving her hands in the air to dry her recently polished nails. She hadn't been able to think of any other way to kill time while nursing her supposed headache.

"You know, that James is a very nice-looking man," Aurora said, "and I think he's rather intrigued with you. He asked a lot of questions about you."

"I hope you told him I have a boyfriend who plays linebacker for the Dolphins."

"Oh, Paige, I told him no such thing. In fact, I made it known that you were quite available. I hope that was all right. Don't you like James?"

"It wasn't all right, and no, I don't particularly like James—at least, not in that way. Please, Mother, stay out of my love life."

"I'm only trying to help," Aurora said, undaunted. "What did you come on this cruise for, if not to meet men?"

To keep you from meeting men. "To relax," she answered as she abruptly stood and began pacing the tiny floor space.

"It doesn't seem to be working."

Paige sat down again. "Give it time," she said, softening. "I've only been on board a few hours. I'll get the hang of it soon."

By the time they headed for the nine-o'clock dinner seating in the elegant Seascape Dining Room, Paige's mood had improved. She felt more like herself in an uncomplicated silk sheath and simple accessories, her unruly hair folded into a sophisticated twist atop her head. She wasn't looking forward to eating shark, no matter who prepared it, but she figured the menu would also include steak or chicken.

Her optimism took an abrupt nosedive when the steward showed them to their table and she saw who else was seated there.

Harrison and James both stood as the ladies approached. "Good evening," Harrison said as he took Aurora's hand between his and gave her a peck on the cheek in an irritatingly debonair gesture.

Who did he think he was, Cary Grant? Paige groused inwardly, although she had to admit he looked the part in his starched white shirt, conservative tie and a charcoal jacket that had obviously been tailored to fit his wide shoulders.

"I hope you don't mind that we arranged to share a table with you," he said.

"We're delighted," Aurora answered smoothly. She looked expectantly at Paige, who remained silent.

The two men and Aurora carried the conversation through most of dinner, sometimes discussing serious topics, other times sharing silly jokes and laughing until their eyes were moist with tears.

No one seemed to mind Paige's pensiveness. Every so often James would lean over and offer an aside to Paige, speaking in a low voice much too near her ear. His warm breath against her cheek, far from provocative, made her want to flee to her cabin and wash her face.

When the waiter set the shark steak in front of her, Paige questioned her impulsive decision to be brave and try something new. What was she trying to prove, anyway? But she ate it without complaint, hardly tasting it, washing it down with the less-than-palatable Chablis from her constantly filled glass.

After dinner Paige considered calling it a night. It was almost eleven. But she had promised Bobby she would keep an eye on Aurora, so she found herself following the others to the Copacabana Lounge. A small orchestra was doing a creditable job on some big band numbers despite its size. Bobby had once sung with a similar band, and a wave of unexpected nostalgia hit her.

"Would you like to dance?" James asked her.

"Umm, no, actually..." she stammered.

"C'mon, Paige," he wheedled. "I'm a terrific ballroom dancer. I'll teach you the steps in no time."

An amused look passed between mother and daughter. If there was one thing Paige didn't need lessons on, it was dancing. Touring the country with her father's band, she had practically grown up in nightclubs, learning everything from the tango to the twist to the Texas two-step.

Harrison was watching her, too, seemingly interested in her response. She felt a sudden, illogical urge to show him that she wasn't completely inept when it came to social skills.

She smiled up at James. "All right, one dance."

The band had just launched into "In the Mood," and she and James fell into an easy jitterbug. James was an adept partner, if not an inspired one, and Paige found that she was almost enjoying herself. They fit well together, James's less-than-towering height complementing her petite size.

"I think you're the one who should be giving lessons," he said when the song ended. "How did you learn to dance like that?"

"My parents taught me," she said, choosing not to elaborate.

The band started a slower number, and James drew her into his arms for a waltz. She wasn't as comfortable dancing so close, and she did her best to maintain some distance between their bodies while James did his best to maximize contact.

She glanced wistfully at their table, wondering how she could end the dance without sounding horribly rude, when she saw Harrison watching them, his black gaze practically burning a hole through her.

Rather than pleasing her, as it should have, the look on his face disturbed her.

Fortunately a beeper in James's coat pocket chose that moment to chirp. "Damn," he said under his breath as he reluctantly released Paige. "Looks like I'll have to go take care of some small emergency. I'll be back as soon as I can."

Paige murmured her insincere regrets over his leaving, breathed a quiet sigh of relief and went back to the table.

"How about it, Aurora?" Harrison was saying, apparently oblivious to Paige's return.

"Oh, I don't think so," Aurora demurred. "I'm not much for dancing, not tonight, anyway. My feet hurt."

What? Paige thought. Since when did her mother not like to dance?

"Besides, I need to go powder my nose," Aurora continued. "If you're set on dancing, why don't you give Paige a try?"

Paige gave a small gasp as they both looked expectantly at her. Dance with Harrison? The mere thought made her dizzy. Or maybe that was just the wine.

"Would you like to dance, Paige?" Harrison asked politely. "If James doesn't mind, that is."

That infuriated her. "James was called away on business," she informed him icily. "But I'm sure he doesn't give a fig whom I dance with, nor would I care if he did."

"Good." Harrison stood and took her hand, urging her out of her chair.

Aurora leaned over to Paige and whispered, "Don't let him dance with anyone else, particularly not that stacked brunette who keeps making cow eyes at him from across the room. I'll be back shortly."

It appeared Paige had no choice but to acquiesce. It irked her that her mother thought her to be far less of a threat than the silicone-implanted bimbo. It irked her again that she even cared.

The band was playing another slow, dreamy number, and Harrison drew her easily into his arms. He was not so skillful a dancer as James, but he was obviously comfortable with his own body and his movements. In moments they were dancing in harmony, despite the height difference between them. He held her not too stiffly, yet not too close, either.

"Could you at least try to appear as if you're enjoying this?" Harrison said. "People will think I'm pulling your fingernails out one by one instead of dancing with you."

Little did he know that he was inflicting a very different brand of torture on her. His nearness caused her body to respond, despite her efforts to remain indifferent. She was acutely aware of his hard, lean torso brushing against hers, the warmth of his hand enveloping hers, the strength of his shoulder where she touched him, the subtle, spicy fragrance of his aftershave.

And the way he looked at her. She could have easily drowned in those brown eyes, which seemed so sincere.

She forced a smile.

"That's a little better. Why do you dislike me so intensely?

"It's habit," she replied, not even bothering to deny the accusation. "I've never liked any of Aurora's suitors. She tends to attract a certain brand of man."

"What if I'm different?" he countered, his hand making slow, sensual circles at the small of her back. "What if I'm gainfully employed, financially secure and a gentleman without designs on Aurora's matrimonial status?''

Paige didn't answer. The feel of his hand, warm and insistent through the silk of her dress, had paralyzed her brain and turned her body into one big nerve ending.

''Well, it's possible, isn't it?'' he prompted.

With no small effort Paige collected her wits. What was she doing? What was she allowing him to do?

''You may be gainfully employed and financially secure,'' she said evenly. ''But a gentleman? For the past few minutes you've been rubbing circles on my back, and now your hand is perilously close to a part of my anatomy that shouldn't be fondled in public. In conclusion, only a cur dog pursues two females at the same time, much less two females who are close to each other. This dance is finished, Mr. Powell. And when I tell Aurora what you're up to, you'll be finished with her, as well.''

Looking a bit startled at her vehement outburst, he dropped his hands, allowing her to escape.

Paige resisted the urge to run. Her face flaming, she left the dance floor, bypassed their table and headed straight for the exit. A detached part of her applauded her blistering speech. Her outrage was perfectly justified; the dressing down was no more than the cad deserved.

But another, more frightened part of herself was forced to admit that she'd liked the way he'd been touching her. For the first time in years she'd felt the full force of her own healthy, feminine response to a man's touch, complete with watery knees, fluttering stomach, heart palpitations and an insistent tug deep in her abdomen, an ache that begged for fulfillment.

If she hadn't willfully summoned up that anger, she would have melted against him, turned her face upward and accepted the kiss she knew had been on his mind.

She probably would have enjoyed it, too.

Three

___

The next morning Paige was determined to put the previous evening's disturbing events behind her. The weather outside was gorgeous, she had a new, sleek, emerald green swimsuit, and the breakfast buffet on the Lido Deck beckoned. After she sated herself, she planned to find a deck chair, an umbrella and several undisturbed hours to lose herself in Stephen King's latest bestseller.

She didn't have to worry about her mother. She'd heard Aurora come dragging in after 2:00 a.m., giggling like a teenager as someone—Paige didn't want to think too hard about who—had walked her to her door. If Aurora was true to form, she wouldn't be out of bed until noon.

Paige did, however, need to borrow Aurora's bottle of sun block. She eased the connecting door open and tiptoed inside her mother's room, where Aurora snored softly, a satin sleeping mask protecting her eyes from the sunlight streaming through the cracks in the curtains.

Now, where would her mother have hidden the suntan lotion? Paige wondered.

"Mmm, Paige?" Aurora said muzzily.

"Sorry, Mother," Paige whispered. "I'm just looking for the sun block."

Aurora leaned up on one elbow and pulled off the mask. "'S in that beach bag . . . oh, there, under the dressing table. Why'd you run off so early last night?" she asked, obviously irritated. "You missed the champagne."

"It wasn't early, it was after midnight," Paige argued amiably. Sooner or later she would have to tell her mother about Harrison's lack of fidelity, but that could wait—at least until Aurora had drunk her first cup of coffee.

"Harrison seemed to think you were miffed at him."

"Oh, he did, did he?"

"Were you?"

Paige weighed her answer carefully. "A bit. You should watch him, Mother. I don't think his intentions are honorable."

"I certainly hope not," Aurora said with a wicked laugh.

"Mother!"

"Oh, Paige, would you lay off the 'Miss Prim' stuff? I'm a grown woman, and I don't need you watchdogging my social life."

"Someone should," Paige muttered.

Aurora chose to ignore the dig. "So where are you off to this morning so disgustingly bright and early?"

Paige was relieved at the change of subject. "To breakfast and then the pool. Want to come?"

Aurora shuddered delicately at the mention of food. "No, thanks, not until I beat this hangover. I'd forgotten what a chipper little morning person you are. Now, go away. I'll see you at a more civilized hour." She shoved the mask back over her eyes and burrowed into the bed covers.

With a shrug Paige grabbed the beach bag, which felt as if it contained a bowling ball, and returned to her own room.

"What in the world is in this thing?" she wondered aloud as she opened the drawstring top and checked out the contents. There were two pairs of sunglasses, a tube of lip balm, under-eye moisturizer, three scarves, and four economy-size bottles of suntan oil, each with a different SPF. The outside zipper pockets held clips to Aurora's electric rollers, a packet of tissues and a costume-jewelry necklace.

Paige examined the necklace. It was pretty, she decided. In fact, she would have thought it was the real thing if she didn't know that stones of this size were well beyond Aurora's means. Still, it was obviously an expensive piece of fakery. She would have to remind Aurora to take better care of it.

Paige laid the necklace on the dresser, intending to return it to her mother later. She selected a few essentials and put them back into the bag, plopped a wide-brimmed straw hat onto her head and headed for the Lido Deck.

"As nearly as we can pinpoint it, the theft occurred between 9:00 p.m. and 1:00 a.m.," James said in a low voice, craning his neck this way and that to be sure there were no eavesdroppers lurking about. He and Harrison were going over the details of the break-in that had occurred last night, proving that the Mermaid cat burglar was on the prowl.

"What exactly was stolen?" Harrison asked.

"A sapphire-and-diamond necklace, worth a cool twenty-seven thousand dollars," James said. "Fortunately the owner isn't the hysterical type. She reported the theft very quietly, and I've convinced her to keep mum so our chief suspect won't know we're on to her. Which leads me to... did you get lucky with Aurora last night?"

Harrison sighed tiredly. "No. An elderly gentleman, a Dr. Waller, walked her back to her cabin at about two. I followed them, then stuck around in the passageway long enough to be sure she didn't take a late-night stroll."

"Then she isn't responsible?" James asked, frowning.

"I didn't say that." Damn, he almost wished he could serve as Aurora's alibi. He was growing fond of her, and it was getting harder and harder for him to believe she was a world-class jewel thief.

What was even harder to swallow was how Paige would handle her mother's arrest. "Aurora went to the ladies' room shortly after you were called away," he admitted. "She was gone more than twenty minutes. I should have followed her, but I didn't. She said she'd be right back, and I didn't think that much of it." He'd been too intent on dancing with Paige to think clearly, anyway.

"Twenty minutes would be enough time, barely," James said, his irritated frown fading. Clearly he was eager to close this case, which had plagued him for more than a year.

"How did the burglar get into the cabin?" Harrison asked.

"A glass cutter was used on the terrace door. It was a clean, quick job. And, Harrison, the cabin that was hit is next door to Aurora's."

"Well, hell, that clinches it, then." Aurora must have climbed over the railing of her veranda and worked her way over to the victim's. Although the woman was fifty-eight years old, she was trim and athletic. The caper wasn't inconceivable. "Any fingerprints?"

"Nope. Like I said, clean and fast."

"Why didn't you tell me as soon as the theft was reported?" Harrison asked.

James's expression hardened. "Silly me. I thought you were making some progress with Aurora, and I didn't want to mess that up. I was hoping you'd get into her cabin and find something useful." He was clearly disgusted with Harrison's lack of success on that front.

"Hey, you think this is easy? Aurora's no pushover."

"That's not what I hear."

All right, so maybe Harrison hadn't tried all that hard, especially when Aurora seemed to be having such a good time with the doctor. "Don't worry, she'll invite me in."

"You know, we could use a passkey. If we knew where the necklace was ahead of time—"

"Forget it," Harrison said, cutting him off. "I work strictly by the book. We can't search without the captain's say-so, and he won't give us that without stronger evidence. So Aurora has to invite me in."

James laughed without humor. "Sometimes I wonder about you, Harrison. I'd be willing to bet I can get into Paige's bed before you get into Aurora's."

Harrison's hand clenched into a fist beneath the table. He longed to punch that self-satisfied smirk off James's face. God, how he hated the other man's attitude. At least Harrison had a halfway defensible reason for romancing Aurora. But James's only motivation for putting the moves on Paige was so he could chalk up another conquest.

"Yeah, the more I think about it," James continued, oblivious to Harrison's suppressed anger, "the more I believe it's essential for me to keep Paige occupied and safely out of the way. Aurora's more likely to tip her hand if she doesn't have to worry about her daughter. Not that Paige is really my type, but she's not half-bad."

Not half-bad? Harrison had to exert excruciating self-control not to lunge for James's throat. Paige Stovall was the sweetest combination of strength and vulnerability Harrison had ever encountered, demurely feminine one minute and fierce as any lioness the next, especially when it came to protecting her mother. Fire and ice. How could anyone think she was less than magnificent?

With a jolt, Harrison realized he was jealous. That's what he'd felt last night, all the way to his gut, when he'd watched Paige dancing with James, laughing with him, touching him. And when Aurora had unwittingly answered his fantasies by practically thrusting Paige into his arms, he'd felt as if the angels had smiled on him. Even though she'd danced with him under protest, he'd enjoyed staring down into those luminous eyes, watching the sparkling night-club lights play against her auburn hair, feeling the firm flesh at the small of her back beneath her silk dress.

She had enchanted him, and he'd completely forgotten himself. It had seemed as natural as breathing to caress her as they danced. It had also been a near-fatal blow to his investigation. He'd have to do a lot of fence mending if he wanted to salvage the operation.

He hadn't confessed that blunder to James. He might still be able to pick up the pieces.

He allowed his hands to relax. It wasn't worth getting thrown off this case just for the satisfaction of breaking James's nose. Besides, there was no reason for him to worry about James getting to Paige. She might be an innocent, but she wasn't stupid.

"Say, speak of the devil, look who's in the buffet line," James said.

Harrison looked, scanning the crowd, uncomfortably eager to catch a glimpse of Paige. There she was, wearing sunglasses and a bulky terry robe that hid her curves, her sun-bright hair tucked beneath a floppy hat. A huge canvas beach bag hung from one shoulder. She was trying to be inconspicuous, no doubt, but he would have recognized those legs anywhere. They might not be terribly long, but they were trim and shapely. For an instant his imagination conjured up an image of those legs wrapped around— No, no, no. He had to stop thinking along those lines.

Aurora, he noticed, was nowhere around.

"Why don't you leave Paige alone?" he said, when he noticed James smoothing his hair and flicking an invisible speck of lint from his razor-creased trousers.

"She doesn't deserve this." But as always, James didn't listen. He quickly made his move, swooping down on Paige like a dive-bomber, picking up her tray from beneath her nose and carrying it back to their table despite her protests.

She had little choice but to follow her breakfast.

"Oh, good morning," she said coolly when she spotted Harrison. "You're up early for having been out so late."

James drew back in surprise. "And just how do you know how late Harrison stayed up?" he asked. Although he appeared to be teasing, there was a hard edge to his question.

"My aunt got back to her cabin after two," she said. "I just assumed she was still with Harrison."

Although she was answering James, she looked straight at Harrison as she spoke. Was she challenging him, daring him to contradict her? Getting into her good graces wasn't going to be easy. Of course, he'd already known that.

"I don't need much sleep," he said pleasantly.

"Would you like me to get you some coffee?" James asked solicitously, helping her remove the plates of fruit, yogurt and muffins from her tray.

"Yes, please,' she said, her voice resigned. "Decaf, black."

James scurried to do her bidding, pausing to tuck her cumbersome beach bag under the table—probably so there would be more room for him to sit close to her.

"Where's Aurora this morning?" Harrison asked.

"I'm afraid she's not feeling well," Paige replied as she reluctantly settled onto the bench opposite him.

She spread margarine onto a blueberry muffin, her eyes impossible to read behind the dark glasses.

"That's terrible," Harrison said. "Has she been to see the ship's doctor?"

"Oh, it's nothing so serious," Paige said. "She's just a little woozy."

A few minutes ago Harrison could have easily believed Aurora was hung over. Last night she'd seemed pretty tipsy when he'd followed her back to her cabin. But that must have been an act, he realized. She would have needed all her wits about her to carry off the theft of the necklace.

The gears in his mind turned furiously. Here was the perfect opportunity to get into Aurora's cabin. "Maybe I should pay her a visit. Does she like flowers? Would that cheer her up?"

He saw the negative answer on Paige's face. But before she could deliver some scathing comment, her expression abruptly softened. "You know, that's really sweet of you. Aurora loves flowers, roses in fact. And chocolates, the kind with nuts in the center. Yes, I think some attention from you would make her feel lots better."

Harrison was skeptical of Paige's sudden change of heart. He would have liked to think he had swayed her with his show of concern, but somehow he didn't think it was that easy.

"You're not just trying to get rid of me, are you?" he asked, snitching a strawberry from her plate despite the fact that he'd hardly touched his own breakfast of eggs and toast.

She surprised him by flashing a mischievous smile and peeking over the top of her sunglasses at him, giving him a heart-stopping glimpse of those amazingly clear green eyes. "Of course not. But if you're going to persist in throwing yourself at Aurora, you might as well do it right."

Had she really decided he wasn't so bad for Aurora? Somehow, that thought didn't cheer him very much.

He was reluctant to leave the table when Paige was feeling more charitable toward him. Especially if James was around. But duty called. He gulped down the last of his coffee, bade her a jaunty good morning and set out on his mission.

Amazingly, he found roses and chocolates, the kind with nuts in the center, in the well-stocked gift shop. Whistling tunelessly, he headed down to the Marlin Deck, acknowledging the smiles of passersby who recognized that he was on a romantic errand.

Suddenly feeling like a complete fraud, he stopped whistling as thoughts of an unpleasant chapter from his past assaulted him. He'd once worked as a criminal defense attorney, and there had been a client, a woman named Kitty Cirello, accused of embezzlement. Kitty had lured him into her bed and convinced him of her love, knowing that if she won him over, he would trade his soul to get her acquitted in court.

That was exactly what he'd done. Afterward, Kitty had admitted her guilt, deliberately making him feel like a fool. The way she'd used him, playing on his emotions to get what she'd wanted, had left a bad taste in his mouth. Right now was he behaving any better?

But I'm the good guy, he tried to convince himself. He was on the side of law and order, and Kitty had been a criminal, just like Aurora.

Did that excuse his behavior?

By the time he knocked on Aurora's door, he was pretty disgusted with himself. Once this assignment was over, he was lowering the boom on his boss—no more undercover work. There was already too much deception in this world without his adding to it.

After what seemed a long time, the door cracked open and one red-rimmed eye peered out at him. "Oh, Lord," Aurora said in a gravelly voice, as she shoved a pair of sunglasses onto her face. "What are you doing here at this ungodly hour?"

"Paige said you weren't feeling well. I thought flowers and candy would cheer you up."

She opened the door another inch to peer at the bouquet of roses and the candy he held. "Dear boy," she said, "there is nothing wrong with me that a few more hours of sleep won't cure. For future reference, I don't socialize before noon. I'm allergic to roses, and I despise chocolate with nuts."

She started to close the door, then paused. "I'm sorry you wasted your money. Don't throw away the candy, though. Paige likes the kind with nuts." She slammed the door, leaving Harrison standing in the passageway feeling like a ninny.

He'd known Paige's sudden affability was too good to be true. He should have smelled the trap. What had happened to his instincts, which his boss had so eloquently bragged about to James Blair?

The only other time he'd lost his ability to think clearly was when he'd been a young, eager attorney, defending Kitty Cirello against what he thought was a gross miscarriage of justice. He had been so wrong about her.

Not that he was wrong about Paige. Oh, she might have a little streak of wickedness in her soul. At least, she wasn't above putting a well-deserved prank over on him. But she wasn't in the same league as Kitty...or her own mother. Still, he resolved to do a better job of keeping his wits about him.

He gave the roses to an elderly woman on the elevator, but he kept the chocolates. Hell, *he* liked the kind with nuts. And he would choke down the entire pound box before he would let Paige have even one.

Paige's morning plans had been shot to hell. First there was her encounter with Harrison, about which she was feeling slightly guilty. Aurora would chew him up and spit him out. Then there was breakfast with James, who had hovered over her like a nervous waiter on his first day while she ate—or tried to eat—her meal. He had stuck to her like lint, just as annoying and just as impossible to shake loose.

She now sat in a deck chair under an umbrella, paperback in hand, but she hadn't made it through a single page. James seemed determined to converse with her, regardless of her broad hints that she wanted to be left alone. She even had to slap his hands away from her beach bag when he tried to dig into it for her sun block, offering to rub some on her back. The prospect gave her more shivers than Stephen King.

Just when she thought things couldn't get any worse, she saw Harrison heading resolutely around the pool in her direction.

Uh-oh, time to pay the piper. By now he would know she'd cheerfully lied to him about Aurora's preferences. She shouldn't have done that. It was childish. But so satisfying.

The expression on Harrison's face as he approached was not the angry one she'd expected. In fact, he looked . . . worried?

"Paige, I'm glad I found you," he said, a touch of restrained urgency in his voice. "Your aunt really isn't feeling well at all, and she asked me to take you back to the cabin."

"Oh, dear," Paige said, tamping down her alarm as she stuffed her book into her beach bag. She'd thought it was just a simple hangover. "Has she seen the doctor?"

"Not yet. Don't panic, I don't think it's anything serious."

"No, probably not," she agreed, allowing Harrison's warm reassurance to calm her. She stood, draping her robe over her shoulder. "Excuse me, James."

"Would you like me to come with you?" James asked.

"No," Paige and Harrison answered in unison.

Harrison escorted Paige out of the pool area and through sliding glass doors that led to the elevators. He paused once they were well out of James's sight. "Wait, I have something to tell you. Aurora's fine. She didn't ask for you."

For a moment all Paige could do was stare at him. Was the man mad as a hatter? "Then why—"

"Because you looked like you needed rescuing, and I couldn't think of a better way to get you away from James."

Paige's jaw dropped. "Of all the . . . if I wanted to get away from James, I'd . . . you scared me, you know. You lied to me."

He gave her a maddeningly superior grin. "Then I'd say we're even."

Oh, yeah. The anger drained out of her, and suddenly the whole thing seemed funny. She laughed, surprising herself. "I *was* getting annoyed with James," she confessed. "Aurora wasn't too hard on you, I hope."

"Aside from nearly breaking my nose when she slammed the door in my face, no, she wasn't too hard."

He seemed to be taking the rejection in stride, Paige thought. "By dinner she will have forgotten all about it," she said. "But she won't be so quick to forgive, once I tell her how you behaved last night. I haven't forgotten."

"Neither have I."

The deep timbre of his voice sent an uncalled-for shiver up her spine. It's just the air-conditioning, she told herself as she slipped into her robe. Surely Harrison didn't still think he could flirt with her to any advantage.

She started to turn away, then paused, unsure where she wanted to go. If she returned to the pool, there was James to contend with. If she went back to her cabin, she might disturb a still-cranky Aurora.

"Have you tried the health club yet?" Harrison asked, as if sensing her quandary. "I was thinking of heading up there. I want to familiarize myself with every aspect of the Mermaid Cruise Line before I invest, and I wouldn't mind getting a woman's opinion of the facilities."

"I'm sure you could find at least a dozen women who would be happy to offer their opinions."

"But none so discerning as you."

The elevator doors opened and she stepped aboard, with Harrison right behind. "Why are you bothering? You know I don't like you."

"I want you to like me," he answered with a degree of honesty Paige found refreshing.

"Why? My mo—" She started again. "My aunt can see whomever she likes, and she doesn't care what I think. She made that very clear this morning."

"I still want you to like me," he repeated. His words, and the way he looked at her with those steady brown eyes, made her heart do a flamenco dance. What game was he playing? And why did she feel this mad compulsion to play it with him?

He punched the button for the Starlight Deck, where the health club was located. She didn't argue with him.

"That's twice you've slipped now," he said with an indulgent smile.

"What do you mean?" She busied her hands by tying her robe tightly about her waist.

"Twice you've almost called Aurora your mother instead of your aunt. But I would have guessed your true relationship, anyway. There's a certain closeness between you that only mothers and daughters share."

Paige sighed, deciding she would come clean. She had never approved of the deception, anyway. "It was Mother's idea. She doesn't want anyone to guess her true age. And please don't let on that you know."

"I won't. But you're one lie up on me now."

"Am I?" She found that idea slightly disturbing. She'd always prided herself on her honesty.

The elevator doors opened onto the health club, with its rich, burgundy carpet and gleaming chrome exercise equipment. Paige had taken only a passing interest in it before, when her mother had taken her on a whirlwind tour of the ship. Now she admired the first-rate facilities. The workout area she frequented at the hospital where she worked wasn't nearly this well equipped, and certainly not this luxurious.

"The ladies' dressing room is that way," Harrison said helpfully. "They provide workout clothes, if you like."

"Mmm, thanks, but I think I'll just settle for a dip in the whirlpool, since I'm already in my suit."

"Great, I'll join you."

"But you don't have a—" Yes, he did, she realized as he reached into the pocket of his shorts and pulled out a tiny scrap of black nylon.

"Be back in a minute."

Terrific, she thought. Not only had she condemned herself to spend the rest of the morning with him, but they would have to share the intimate confines of the hot tub, and him nine-tenths naked.

In the men's locker room, Harrison went over and over his rationalization for what he was about to do. His plan to romance Aurora was failing miserably. The woman might be an accomplished flirt, but she was not seriously interested in him, and she wasn't going to get chummy enough to allow him into her cabin. As a matter of fact, he got the distinct impression that the distinguished doctor would get the nod from Aurora long before Harrison.

All was not lost, however. It hadn't escaped Harrison's attention that Aurora had been subtly pushing him toward her daughter. It might be time to focus his attentions on Paige. If he got in good with the daughter, he still had an excuse to stick close to Aurora and either observe her in the midst of a theft or find incriminating evidence in her room. She and Paige were sharing a suite, after all.

His new plan was tantalizingly attractive. He certainly wouldn't have to depend on his theatrical abilities. At the same time, it filled him with distaste. He would be using Paige. And even if he did manage to win her over—no small task—in the end he would end up destroying whatever developed between them. He would coax her into trusting him, and then blow her fragile trust to smithereens.

Just like Kitty had done to him.

But I'm the good guy, he reminded himself again. This was his job. Short of bailing out, damaging his firm's reputation and probably losing his job, he had no choice but to do what he must to catch his thief.

Four

There were two hot tubs, one inside and one on deck, and Paige chose the one outside because it was bigger, less intimate. However, although it was roomy enough to seat at least ten people, an older lady in a bathing cap was the only occupant when Paige approached. The woman looked up and smiled toothily. "Come on in, the water's fine—if you enjoy feeling like a stewed tomato."

Paige smiled back. The crystal clear water, steaming lightly, did look inviting. She dipped a toe in to test the temperature, finding it a little warmer than she'd expected.

"You'll like it once you get used to it," the other woman assured her. "I, however, am going to be parboiled if I don't get out pretty soon." She placed a hand on the edge of the tub for support and hoisted herself onto her feet.

"Oh, you're not leaving, are you?" Paige asked, feeling a slight edge of panic.

The woman smiled kindly. "I'd love to stay and chat, but I'm meeting my husband in a few minutes for a walk about the deck." She climbed out of the tub and grabbed her beach towel. "Don't worry, I'm sure someone else will be along anytime now."

That's just what Paige was afraid of. Any moment Harrison would arrive in those indecently small swimming trunks, and here she would be, a little stewed tomato waiting to be devoured. She waved a distracted farewell to the woman, then took off her robe and hat and eased herself into the bubbling water.

It did feel good, she decided, as she found a seat on the shady side of the tub and immersed herself up to the neck. She leaned her head back and closed her eyes, clearing her mind.

She was aware of Harrison the moment he arrived, although he made no sound. Resisting the urge to open her eyes and look at him in that itty-bitty swimsuit, she instead forced her expression to remain placid, as if his nearness did not affect her.

Her imagination, however, was almost worse than the real thing. She pictured him sliding into the warm water, his leg muscles flexing, his chest tan and rippling. Did he have a lot of hair on his chest? she wondered.

She knew exactly when he moved to sit next to her, because she caught a whiff of his after-shave mingling with chlorine and sunshine.

"There's room for a circus in this tub," she said, still without opening her eyes. "Must you sit right next to me?"

"The sun would be in my eyes on the other side."

"A weak excuse if ever I heard one." Finally she peeped through her eyelids, startled to find his face so close to hers. Oh, those eyes, so brown and velvety, like a deer's. Only a lot more dangerous. "Don't you have any scruples?"

"What do you mean?"

"I mean you're a hopeless cad, and you're never going to get either Aurora or me into bed," she blurted out.

"Paige..." He ran a wet finger down her bare arm, sending shivers all the way to her toes despite the water's warmth. "I have no intention of taking your mother to bed, and I never did."

"Right," she said on a huff. She closed her eyes again, finding it difficult to maintain her skepticism when he was looking at her that way, so sincere, so... believable.

"I won't deny that Aurora is a charming woman. She draws attention to herself, and men just naturally respond, myself included. But it was all in innocence. The more time I spent with the two of you, the more I realized that you're the one I'm interested in. Your charm is much more subtle than your mother's, but much more potent, at least to me. I'm sorry it took me so long to see that."

"Charm, huh?" She opened her eyes again and, finding him uncomfortably close, scooted several inches away. "I've been about as charming as a pit bull with PMS."

He trailed his finger down her arm again and grinned wickedly. "Sexiest pit bull I ever saw."

Paige's heart slammed into her chest, and her lungs contracted. What was this man doing to her? And why did she feel so helpless to combat it? Sure, his attentions were flattering, but that was no reason to let him melt her into acquiescent goo.

"I suppose it was completely innocent when you stayed out till 2:00 a.m. with Aurora, drinking champagne."

"I believe that was Doc Waller who bought and shared the champagne with Aurora. He's the one who walked her back to her cabin, too."

"Oh." That took some of the oomph out of her argument. "Look, Harrison," she said, trying to sound firm. But her voice shook. "Even if your line of baloney were to impress me, which it doesn't, I am not in competition with my mother. She saw you first, she has her eye on you, and I'm not about to get in the middle. Have I made myself perfectly clear on that p-p—" Her speech stumbled to a halt. Harrison touched her face, turning her toward him. He leaned closer, and she realized in one blindingly clear flash that he was going to kiss her.

He can't do that, her mind protested. Hadn't he heard a word she'd just said? But somehow the protests never made it to her lips, at least not before Harrison's mouth did. She drew a ragged breath, intending to say something—anything. But he closed the distance between them and she was lost.

His kiss was better than anything she could have dreamed up, warm and firm and emotionally moving in a way no mere kiss should have been. It robbed her of all good sense and willpower and everything else she prided herself on. It stole her peace of mind, what little there'd been, as well as the air from her lungs.

Before she could stop herself she wound her arms around his neck, craving a more intimate touch, delightedly shocked at how firm his neck and shoulders were. He dug his fingers into her damp hair, pulling it from the single clip that had held it up off her neck. The soft strands tickled her bare shoulders.

In one smooth movement he pulled her almost-weightless body into his lap. His kiss grew more insistent, his mouth moving hungrily against hers, his tongue seeking entrance while his hands roamed at will over her back. She opened her mouth and accepted the intimate invasion, all the time chanting silently, *This is crazy. This is crazy.* But she couldn't deny the kernel of pure, unadulterated happiness that was blooming inside her. This man had an effect on her like nothing she'd experienced.

A foreign noise invaded Paige's consciousness. She realized too late it was the sliding glass door from the health club opening, followed by a surprised gasp and the unmistakable sound of someone making a panicked retreat. The intrusion brought her back to her senses, and she forced herself to end this insanity. With no small effort she pushed herself away and clamored off Harrison's lap, nearly dunking her head in the process.

"You really are good at this, you know?" she said, looking anywhere but at him. Still, she couldn't help but notice he did have a lot of hair on his chest—dark brown, springy curls that glistened with water droplets.

He grinned. "So I've been told."

"That wasn't meant as a compliment. I could never trust a man who could launch such a practiced seduction." Actually it was herself she didn't trust. She moved completely across the hot tub from him, out of touching distance.

His smile faded. "I'm not trying to seduce you, Paige. I just wanted to kiss you. I've wanted to since last night. I'm not trying to get you into bed."

"Ha!"

"Okay, maybe that's not the farthest thing from my mind right now," he conceded. "But I want to get to know you. And I want you to get to know me. Are you afraid you'll find out I'm not such a bad guy after all?"

"I know exactly what kind of guy you are—the kind who'll take advantage of any opportunity, the kind who'll say whatever he thinks it will take to get a woman into bed. A . . . a gigolo! Well, you can take your hairy chest and your deer's eyes and ply someone else with them, 'cause I'm not buying!" With that she stood and made a lunge for the ladder. She had to get out of here, before she succumbed to passion again. She grabbed her hat and her robe, then had to turn back when she forgot her beach bag. She made yet another ungainly exit, nearly slipping on the wet tile around the hot tub, only this time she got the distinct impression that Harrison was not amused.

Hairy chest and deer's eyes? Harrison pulled himself out of the hot tub, too, but he didn't give chase. He'd done enough damage for one morning.

She was right. In his eagerness to press the small advantage he'd imagined with Paige, he'd pushed himself on her, throwing out B movie come-on lines. That wasn't like him. If not for the time constraint he was working under, he would have pursued her in a very different fashion—slowly, cautiously, giving her time to figure out that he wasn't some fast-talking gigolo.

In his mind's eye he could see them sharing late-night walks on the beach, or maybe splitting a pizza and a six-pack of beer at the drive-in movie. And then, when she didn't stiffen every time he touched her, when she didn't eye him with skepticism every time he said something personal, when she didn't question his every motive, then he would kiss her, and not before. That's how he wished he could have orchestrated his seduction of Paige Stovall.

Too late now, he thought grimly. Sure, she'd responded to his kiss in a big way, pressing herself against him like a suddenly affectionate cat eager for a good scratch. But that had been her hormones talking, not her brain. And something told him that Paige seldom let anything override that quick mind of hers.

Hell, he'd blown it this time. He might as well confess to James right now that his plans to stick close to Aurora had failed miserably. He would never get inside her cabin now. He had a feeling the two women were about to close ranks against him.

Maybe it was just as well. This whole assignment was becoming extremely distasteful. Let some other poor fool arrest Aurora and tear mother and daughter apart.

As she rode the elevator down to the Marlin Deck, Paige blotted herself dry as best she could with her terry robe, then shrugged into it and belted it tightly, as if that could fend off her memories of that kiss. Why had she allowed it to happen? And how was she going to explain things to Aurora?

She couldn't put it off any longer. Her mother had to be told in no uncertain terms that Harrison Powell wasn't worth her time.

Again she wondered: Had she done something to deliberately draw Harrison to her? Had she, on some subconscious level, been trying to prove to herself and Aurora that she could beat her own mother at seduction? But as she scrutinized her behavior, she couldn't say she'd done anything to encourage him. But she had succumbed to his potent masculinity, if only briefly. Was that so wrong? What sane woman wouldn't weaken momentarily when a man like Harrison pressed himself on her?

That didn't make her feel any less guilty. She couldn't wait to tell Aurora and get the whole thing off her conscience.

When she knocked softly on the connecting door to Aurora's room, she got a cheery "Come in!" Sounded like her mother's hangover was history.

"Did you have a good morning?" Aurora asked. She was seated at the dresser, applying her false eyelashes.

"It was a . . . different morning. I'm sorry about Harrison showing up with the roses and candy. That was my fault," Paige admitted.

"You think I didn't see your fingerprints all over that one? Really, Paige, that wasn't very nice."

"Well, *he's* not very nice," she said hotly. "In fact, he's a two-timing jerk, and I don't think we should have anything more to do with him."

Aurora looked up in surprise, one eyelash half-glued and sticking out comically. "Now why do you say that?"

"Because, when you're not around, he's chasing other women."

"Other women?" Aurora repeated.

"One other woman, okay? He's a low-life, pond-scum-sucking— Oh, Mother, I'm sorry to break the news to you like that. But you needed to know."

Aurora laughed. "Paige, darling, Harrison can chase anyone he wants. There's nothing between him and me except a little innocent flirtation. That's the way this game is played. You cast out your lures, see who nibbles, then make your choice. I have to admit I enjoy him immensely, but don't you think he's a bit young for me?"

Paige was floored. She'd never heard her mother admit that any man was too young for her. "He's older than Pablo," she said, Pablo being a certain conga player to whom her mother had once been briefly married.

Aurora smiled fondly. "Ah, yes, Pablo. What a charmer. All right, we can both agree that Pablo was an unfortunate choice on my part. Maybe I've learned something. As a matter of fact . . . I'm rather enjoying Doc Waller. He might be older than me, but he can sure shake a leg on that dance floor. Are you surprised?"

Surprised wasn't the word. *Flabbergasted* maybe? "Who walked you to your door last night?" Paige asked suspiciously.

"Why, Doc did, of course." She laughed. "Oh, you thought Harrison did? No, no, darling. So, who's he chasing? Don't tell me he's after that implanted brunette. I thought he had better taste."

"No, it's not her he's after." Paige paused and flopped down on the bed. "It's me."

Aurora's mouth dropped open and she stared at Paige in the dresser mirror. "You're kidding."

Paige drew herself up. "Is it so impossible to believe?"

"Well, no, of course not. It's just that you haven't exactly encouraged him."

"Apparently he likes a challenge."

A slow smile spread over Aurora's face. "Well, well, this is an interesting development. I told you the salt air has a beneficial effect on the libido." She abandoned her eyelashes for the moment and joined Paige on the bed. "I want to know everything. What did he say? What did he do? What did you do?"

"You mean, you aren't upset?"

Aurora appeared puzzled. "Why would I be upset that my daughter has found a man, and a yummy one at that?"

It took a few moments for Paige to adjust her thinking. So Harrison hadn't committed mortal sin, at least by Aurora's standards. When he'd flirted with Aurora, he'd merely been "casting out lures." And he'd made his choice. He wanted Paige.

He wanted her. "Oh, holy cheese, I really blew it this time."

"Blew what?" Then comprehension dawned on Aurora's face. "Oh, Paige, what did you do?"

"I called him a gigolo," she admitted sheepishly.

Aurora's mouth dropped open, but then she snapped it shut, suddenly assuming an eminently practical air. "Okay, so you had a little spat. That doesn't mean all is lost. You still have plenty of time to repair the damage. Go get in the shower while I put together an outfit for you. We'll do your makeup, your hair—"

"Mother, no," Paige said firmly. "If Harrison could be moved by makeup and clothes and perfume, he'd have gone for the brunette. Anyway, I don't want to entice him. I think I should just leave well enough alone."

"But you can't," Aurora said. "The man is smitten with you, and you insulted him. You have to at least apologize. You don't want him to think you're cruel and heartless, do you?"

Paige considered fibbing, telling her mother that she really didn't care what Harrison thought of her. But she did. In a big way. Even when she'd believed him to be the worst sort of villain, she'd still been drawn to him. There was a certain innate kindness in him, an ability to see beneath the skin, that she'd never encountered in a man before. At the very least, she owed him an apology. She nodded.

"All right, then," Aurora said. "He's worth a bit of effort. At least get changed for lunch. And be thinking of how you'll apologize." She moved back to the dresser and started over with the eyelashes.

Paige knew that for once she should follow her mother's advice. She had said some awful things to Harrison, things he didn't really deserve, and she had to set things right. But as for actually encouraging his attentions...

"Mother, why would I want to get involved with a man who lives... my gosh, I don't even know where he lives. We'll never see each other after the cruise is over."

Aurora smiled wickedly. "Silly girl. He happens to live in New York, but there's no law that says he has to stay there. Or that you have to stay in Miami."

Despite telling herself it didn't matter, Paige had showered and dressed with extra care, choosing an emerald green, washable silk blouse and a short denim skirt imprinted with flowers. She even dabbed on a bit of perfume. But her preparations were for nothing. Harrison was nowhere to be found during lunch, nor did he make an appearance the rest of the afternoon. She even asked James if he'd seen Harrison. But James, in an unusually snappish mood himself, replied that he had no idea where Harrison had disappeared to. Then he'd muttered something about people who didn't follow through on their promises, causing Paige to wonder if Harrison had decided he wouldn't invest in Mermaid Cruise Line after all.

Feeling deflated, she decided to take an aerobics class before dinner. Although the food on this cruise was fabulous and plentiful, she was determined she wasn't going to leave the ship with more pounds than when she boarded. So she donned a rather skimpy leotard and headed for the Lido Deck, where a perky little thing with a gratingly high voice led the class in a series of strenuous dance steps.

Paige was a regular at her hospital's aerobics classes, so she had no trouble keeping up. Still, by the end of the hour, she was sweaty and winded and generally disheveled. Of course, that was when she ran into Harrison. She spotted him leaning against the railing, staring out at the vast ocean. The early evening sun on his lean face and the wind ruffling his hair made her think of a sea captain from a bygone era.

Her first instinct was to escape. She was a mess! But when might she catch him alone again? She'd been thinking long and hard about what she wanted to say to him, and this was the perfect opportunity. Anyway, she told herself for the umpteenth time, it didn't matter if he thought she was unkempt. The important thing was to make that apology. Then, if she knew what was good for her, she'd get as far away from him as possible. Thrusting her chin forward, she walked resolutely toward him.

"Hi, Harrison. What are you doing?"

He turned to look at her, mildly surprised, if his expression was any indication. But he didn't give much away. "Oh, I was just plotting my next seduction, you know. Gigolo stuff."

Ouch. Okay, she deserved that. Her first instinct was to come back with a smart line. But then she looked into his eyes, and what she saw there took her breath away. Pain. She'd hurt him. It boggled her mind that she had the ability to inflict pain on a man like Harrison. It was even worse to realize she'd done so, and quite deliberately, too, although at the time she'd figured he would simply move on to his next attempted conquest.

"I'm sorry, Harrison," she said, coming closer to him. "After I talked with Mother, I realized everything you told me was the truth. You might be a hopeless flirt, but...but I guess there's nothing horribly wrong with that." All right, so it wasn't the most gracious apology in the world.

He said nothing. He simply stared at her, his gaze boring into her.

"You have to understand," she continued, wanting to fill the awkward silence. "I'm very sensitive about...about competing with my mother. It happened once before, and it's not an experience I care to repeat."

"Really?" Finally the ghost of a smile touched his lips. "You stole Aurora's boyfriend? Tell me about it."

"Oh, I couldn't," she said, not bothering to correct his misconception. "It was all very silly, and a long time ago. But it put a strain on our relationship, and that's much too important to trifle with. I'm very close to Aurora, and I wouldn't hurt her for the world."

"Yes, I can see that. You wouldn't let anyone else hurt her, either."

"That's why I came on this cruise to begin with—to watch out for her." Before she knew it, she was telling him all about Aurora's succession of inappropriate husbands, her tendency to run amok whenever she took a cruise and Bobby's insistence that Paige somehow prevent marriage number five.

"Daddy said he would pull the plug on Aurora's finances if she married again," Paige confessed. They'd begun to stroll along the deck. "Every time she gets married, she ends up turning to my dad to bail her out. And he does. He still looks out for her, financially and in other ways, even though they've been divorced for twelve years. Mother needs him. I can't stand the thought of him turning his back on her once and for all."

"Do you really think he'd do that?" Harrison asked.

Reluctantly she nodded. "He was pretty mad when he found out Aurora was taking another cruise. I've never seen him like that, not even during the divorce. He said if she walks down the aisle again, he's done with her. And I think he means it." She sighed.

"What broke them up?" Harrison asked.

Paige shrugged. "Who knows? They were both a little restless, I think, after twenty-five years of marriage. They'd struggled through most of those years while Daddy tried to make it in the entertainment business. When he finally sold a couple of songs and the money started rolling in, our life-style changed dramatically. I'm not sure either of my parents knew how to handle success.''

She paused at the railing to look out at the inky blue sea, composing her thoughts. "Funny, but sometimes when you get what you've dreamed of all your life, you find out it doesn't cure all your problems like you thought it would. It doesn't make you happy."

Harrison stopped beside her, close but not touching. He knew all about the kind of disillusionment Paige was talking about. He'd gone through law school full of idealism, ready to battle injustice and champion the underdog.

It had taken him exactly two months in private practice to come to the conclusion that there was no justice meted out in the court system. The guy with the most money and the best lawyer usually won. The criminal with the best angle went free while another, perhaps less knowledgeable about the legal system, went to jail.

Kitty Cirello had been his salvation—or so he'd thought. There had been his chance to make a difference, to right the injustice of an innocent woman falsely accused. What a jerk he'd been. He'd felt so flattered when Kitty had specifically chosen him to defend her in court. But he'd been selected not for his brilliance, but his gullibility. Kitty had known she could wrap him around her little finger and involve him emotionally in her cause.

"I can't believe how I've just been rattling on," Paige said. "I wanted to talk about you and me, not about my parents."

"Is there a 'you and me'?" he asked, amazed at how quickly he was willing to forgive her for thinking the worst of him. He wanted to touch her, to somehow reaffirm the tenuous bond that had formed between them. But he resisted, leery of scaring her away. He would not make the same mistake twice.

"I'd like—" Paige started, then cut herself off. She looked up at him, her green eyes sparkling like gems in the sun, yet full of uncertainty. Then a mischievous smile began tugging at the corners of her mouth, and before he could guess what she was up to, she stood on tiptoes and pressed a quick, shy kiss to his mouth.

Harrison's whole body went hard at the feel of her soft, yielding lips against his and the sweet, musky smell of her, brought on by whatever she'd been doing in that leotard before she'd stumbled into him. He resisted the urge to pull her closer for a proper kiss, worried that the force of his desire would make mincemeat of her attempt to make up with him.

"I guess there is a you and me," he murmured, pressing his face into her hair. In the back of his mind, a voice reminded him that he still had a job to do, and Paige Stovall had just handed him a golden opportunity. He was back in her good graces, and Aurora's, as well, it seemed. He could yet get into their cabin and search for the stolen necklace, or for whatever gear Aurora had used to climb over her balcony railing and onto the veranda next door.

The voice also reminded him that he was still lying to Paige, using Paige.

"Oh, shut up," he murmured.

Paige drew back and looked at him. "Pardon me?"

"Nothing," he said. "Nothing at all."

Paige and Harrison walked around the Starlight Deck for a while in companionable silence. But Paige was breathlessly aware of his nearness, disturbed by her escalating reaction to him.

She was in over her head. Shipboard flings simply weren't her style, yet how could anything more serious possibly develop? Despite Aurora's optimism, Paige couldn't imagine Harrison getting serious enough in a week's time to want to continue their relationship after they disembarked.

But somewhere deep inside her, Paige held on to a hope for just that. She could get really serious, really fast, when she knew good and well she'd be setting herself up for another heartbreak. Was she crazy? Or was she destined to repeat her mother's mistakes, falling for every handsome guy she met on the deck of a ship? She had always thought Aurora weak for being such a victim to her hormones and her runaway heart. Now, for the first time, Paige understood what it felt like to lose control of her own feelings, and she felt more sympathy for her mother.

Her musings came to an abrupt halt when she and Harrison rounded a corner and ran smack into James. Immediately self-conscious, she stepped away from Harrison, as if to make it clear they were not a couple.

"Hello, James," she said, knowing she sounded overly bright.

James offered her a brittle smile. "Paige. I was just speaking to your aunt. She seems to have made a miraculous recovery."

Paige cast a guilty glance over at Harrison, then back to James. "Well, you know how it is with seasickness. That medicine works wonders." She wasn't actually lying, she reasoned. She never specifically said Aurora had been seasick.

"I thought you were the one with that particular malady," James said.

Paige cleared her throat. "Haven't been bothered with it myself on this trip."

James stared at her, challenging, for one agonizingly long second, before turning his attention to Harrison. "Harrison, the captain would like a word with you right away. There are some features on the bridge he'd like to demonstrate."

Harrison smiled pleasantly. "Sounds interesting. Paige, have you visited the bridge yet?"

She started to answer, but James interrupted. "Sorry, Paige, but the bridge is a restricted area. Only those invited by the captain are allowed access."

"Then we'll get her invited," Harrison said with a shrug.

"No, really, that's okay," Paige said, feeling more ill at ease with each passing second. "I don't want to cause any trouble, and besides, I need to get dressed for dinner. I'll see you both later." Why was she always making these awkward escapes? she wondered. But when she glanced at Harrison, he winked at her. The decidedly suggestive twinkle in his eyes caused a pleasurable shiver to skitter along her back. She quickly waved and walked away, leaving the two men alone.

"What in the hell is going on?" James demanded, the moment Paige was out of earshot. "You're supposed to be working on the suspect, not dallying with the daughter. I thought we agreed I would take care of Paige."

Harrison bit his tongue to keep from verbally flaying James up one side and down the other. He wasn't in the habit of having to explain himself every five minutes when he was working on an investigation. "In case you hadn't noticed, James, our plan wasn't working. Aurora would no more let me into her cabin than she would a cobra. But Paige, on the other hand, is coming along just fine. And if you hadn't interrupted, I would have made plans with her for tonight."

"What good will it do you to get into her cabin?" James asked with a petulant frown. "I doubt she knows anything."

Harrison could think of several answers to that question, all of them pleasurable. But those weren't the answers James was looking for. "There's a connecting door between their two cabins," he said. "I'll get through it ... somehow. Is the captain really expecting me on the bridge?"

"No more than Aurora was expecting to see her daughter this morning," James said smugly, obviously pleased that he'd caught on to Harrison's and Paige's little charade. "What was that all about, anyway?"

"I needed to talk to Paige, and you were monopolizing her." Harrison didn't elaborate.

"Well, the captain is expecting you to sit at his table tonight. I thought it would look fishy if he ignored you during the whole cruise."

"That's no problem. I assume I'm allowed to bring a guest?"

"I was counting on Aurora dining with you. I suppose she's not who you had in mind?"

Harrison shook his head.

"And who's supposed to keep an eye on our suspect?"

"I don't see why you can't do that."

"I'm not being paid to watch Aurora. You are."

Harrison was tired of arguing with the little twerp. "Look, I'm being paid to catch a thief, and I'm going about it the best way I know how. Now either let me do things my own way or hire another investigator."

"Fine," James said, his voice clipped. "I'll let you explain to the captain about the progress you've made—or lack thereof." His deck shoes squeaked as he pivoted on his heel and stalked away.

Harrison shook his head. He'd boxed himself into a helluva corner, but he could see no way out. He was just going to have to play with the cards he'd been dealt and see the hand through to its conclusion.

Five

Harrison Powell was as tenacious as a burr, Paige thought as she sat in one of the *Caribbean Mermaid*'s lounges and let the smoky sounds of jazz pour over her. He was determined to woo her, and she was just as determined not to be overwhelmed by his charm. If anyone were keeping score, however, they would have to conclude that Harrison was winning.

Paige had wanted to tell him no when he'd called earlier that evening and asked her to dine with him at the captain's table. Ever since she'd left him on deck, she'd been steeling herself to use common sense where Harrison was concerned. They had come to a certain understanding, that was all. No need for her to fall at his feet, just because she no longer believed him to be a cad.

But her willpower had failed her once again, and she'd agreed to have dinner with him, provided Aurora was invited, too. No matter how flattered Paige was over Harrison's attentions, she couldn't lose sight of her responsibility to watch over her mother. Besides, with her mother around as a reminder, it was easier for Paige to resist getting swept away.

After dinner Doc Waller had joined them, along with a nice older couple from Dallas, Dan and Thelma Janks, who were friends of Doc's. They'd all wandered into this lounge for after-dinner drinks, and Paige had to admit it was one of the more pleasant interludes she'd had since boarding the ship the previous morning. Even when James found them and invited himself to join their party, Paige didn't mind, although the curious tension she'd sensed earlier between James and Harrison was now almost palpable.

Surely she wasn't the cause. No two men had ever fought over her.

"My, that is a lovely ring," Aurora was saying to Thelma Janks. "May I see it?"

"Oh, certainly." Thelma removed the ring, which sported a huge green stone, and handed it to Aurora. "Dan gave it to me for our thirtieth anniversary. It's a Brazilian emerald."

Harrison and James, who were both paying attention to the exchange, shared a look of silent understanding that baffled Paige.

"It's lovely," Aurora said breathlessly, holding the ring up to the light. "I have a weakness for emeralds." Almost reluctantly, it seemed, she handed the ring back to Thelma.

Paige felt a stab of melancholy. Bobby had given Aurora an emerald ring for some anniversary or other. It was the first piece of really fine jewelry Aurora had ever owned, and she had treasured it. But shortly before the divorce, during one of their stormy arguments, she had pulled the ring off in a fit of pique and thrown it at Bobby. Bobby had calmly picked it up off the floor and put it in his pocket. He'd never given it back.

Paige wondered if her mother was remembering that other ring, because she grew unusually pensive.

Thelma stood and stretched. "Well, Dan, shall we take a stroll on the deck before we turn in?" she asked.

Dan nodded, and they said their good-nights and left.

"And I have some work to take care of before I turn in," James said hastily.

"You know, I think I'll call it a night, too," Aurora said. "I've got a bit of a headache, and I'd like to be rested for our day in Cozumel tomorrow."

"I'll walk you back to your cabin," Doc said.

Paige felt another small ripple of panic, and she opened her mouth to announce that she was retiring, too. She really shouldn't let Doc and Aurora return to the suite alone. But her panic had more to do with the fact that if she stayed, she and Harrison would be alone.

Who knew what temptations awaited her? All night long she'd been thinking about the passionate kiss they'd shared in the hot tub, wondering what might have happened if she hadn't pulled back...wondering if and when she would pull back next time he launched a similar assault.

If he wanted to make love to her, would she agree? It was utter foolishness to become intimate with a man she'd just met, and one she'd likely never see again once the cruise was over. But the temptation was strong.

She looked over at Harrison, wondering what was going through his mind. But his thoughts apparently weren't running along the same line as Paige's. In fact, he was ignoring her altogether, staring after Aurora's retreating form, his expression pensive, maybe even worried.

The jazz quartet, which had been taking a break, started up again. Paige touched Harrison's arm. "Harrison? Do you want to dance?"

He looked at her distractedly. "Uh, I would, but... I'm kind of tired myself. I think I'll pack it in, too. Would you excuse me?"

Paige realized it wouldn't have mattered if she hadn't excused him. He brushed a quick kiss against her lips and was gone before she could even open her mouth to object.

"Well I'll be damned," she said, folding her arms and slumping back in her chair. Here she was, weaving romantic fantasies about Harrison like some smitten schoolgirl, when apparently he had his mind on something—or someone—much more pressing. Like Aurora, maybe?

Oh, for heaven's sake. Paige had to stop allowing her insecurities to gain the upper hand. Harrison and Aurora had both made it clear to her they weren't romantically interested in each other. But she couldn't help wondering why Harrison, so attentive to her all evening long, had suddenly found thoughts of going to bed—alone—so alluring.

"Hurry up, Mother, we're going to miss the launch." Paige sat on Aurora's bed. She'd been dressed and ready for an hour or more, having awakened early and full of energy despite lying awake last night, getting tangled up in the sheets and mercilessly punching her pillow.

The *Caribbean Mermaid* had docked at Cozumel just before dawn, and Paige was looking forward to leaving the blasted ship for a day of sight-seeing. She was also looking forward to some much-needed distance from Harrison—especially after last night.

"Your hair looks fine," she told Aurora, waving at the cloud of hair-spray filling the cabin. "Let's go."

Aurora gave her platinum blond cap one final spritz. "Will you relax? We have plenty of time. I don't see how you can be so vivacious at this hour of the morning. Of course, rumor has it that falling in love gives you lots of energy." She flashed her daughter a sly smile.

"Really, Mother, I'm not anywhere close to falling in love," Paige huffed. "In fact, I'm looking forward to spending the day away from Harrison. His presence is slightly... overwhelming."

"Mmm, and I trust you'll be overwhelmed soon. Only five days left of the cruise. Time's a-wasting."

Paige shook her head. It was no use arguing with Aurora, who threw herself into romantic affairs with total abandon, no thought to the consequences, and expected everyone else to do the same.

Paige had found herself dangerously close to that mind-set last night—which was why she wanted to spend the day away from Harrison. She needed to climb off cloud nine, gather her wits and decide exactly how far she wanted this—this flirtation to go.

Unfortunately her plans went awry. As she and Aurora were waiting in line to board the tender boat that would take them to shore, a strong pair of hands encircled her waist from behind, and a low, sexy voice whispered in her ear.

"Thought I'd never find you in this crowd."

"Harrison! What are you doing here?"

Aurora frowned at her daughter's less-than-gracious greeting.

"I mean, I'm just surprised to see you," Paige amended. "I thought you'd spend the day looking at the bilge pump, or whatever it was Captain Barnes was talking about last night. You seemed awfully interested in it."

"I can think of a few more interesting things than a state-of-the-art bilge pump," he said with an easy smile. "I've never been to Cozumel. Besides, I want to experience what the average passenger does."

"Is that part of your investigation?" Paige asked.

He looked startled at her question, uncomfortably so, though Paige couldn't imagine why. Then his smile returned. "I'm nothing if not thorough," he said, squeezing her shoulder. "Say, isn't that Doc over there?"

At the mention of Doc's name, Aurora's eyebrows flew up and she scanned the crowd, quickly zeroing in on her prey. "Yoo-hoo! Doc! We're over here."

"Nice going," Paige said to Harrison in an undertone. "I'm trying to keep my mother's mind off men, and you're playing matchmaker."

"But Doc seems like such a nice guy," Harrison argued. "Are you sure he'd be all that bad for your mother?"

Paige sighed. "He's better than some of the others. But after what my dad said . . . I just don't want to see Mother rush into marriage again. She's like a teenager when it comes to romance, all hormones and no sense at all.''

''Well, even if Aurora wants to rush things, perhaps Doc doesn't. I think it'll work out okay.''

A light went on in Paige's mind. ''Harrison, that's a marvelous idea.''

He looked confused. ''Excuse me? I think I lost something there.''

''You talk to Doc, and find out what his intentions are. If he's not interested in marriage, it'll really put my mind at ease.''

Harrison frowned. ''I think we should stay out of it. They're adults, after all.''

''Please, Harrison? Just bring up the subject casually if you get a chance. You don't have to interrogate him.''

Reluctantly he nodded. ''All right. But you'll owe me. And I think I'll enjoy collecting.'' He laid his hand casually at the back of her neck, rubbing lazy circles on her nape with his thumb, beneath her hair where no one could see.

She ducked away, uncomfortable with the possessive gesture. Just the same, the mere brush of his fingertips against her sensitive skin made her shivery with pleasure.

The trip to shore didn't help at all. The *Mermaid*'s passengers were packed like sardines into the small boat, and Paige found herself and Harrison pressed together like two spoons in a drawer. He put his hands on her shoulders and pulled her back even closer, seeming to enjoy the intimate contact.

Paige might have enjoyed it, too, if she weren't suddenly so aware of the stifling heat, the stuffy air and the fact that she couldn't see outside the boat. She hadn't taken her motion sickness pills this morning, figuring she'd soon be on dry land, but she hadn't counted on this claustrophobic, floating sardine can.

"Paige? You okay?" Harrison asked, apparently aware of her distress.

"I, uh, not really," she admitted, twisting her head around to look up at him. "It's so... hot." She could feel beads of perspiration breaking out on her forehead.

"You're seasick?" he said, turning a bit pale himself.

Paige couldn't blame him. He was probably imagining the disaster of her actually getting sick in this crowd. She took several deep breaths. She was absolutely not going to embarrass herself. "I'm just a little queasy," she said, understating her distress.

He lifted the heavy mass of her hair off her neck and blew gently on her nape. "You'll be okay," he said. "Take some more deep breaths. That's it. We'll reach the dock soon."

Paige closed her eyes. Whatever he was doing, it was working. The nausea receded, the dizziness abated. She was going to be fine. Still, she had to hold herself back from stampeding to the hatch when the boat finally did dock. The moment she saw daylight, she drank in great lungfuls of fresh air.

"That," she said, casting a baleful eye toward the small orange boat, "is an instrument of torture. I don't suppose I could swim back to the ship when we're finished for the day?"

Harrison gave her an indulgent smile. "You did fine. We'll make sure you get to ride above deck on the way back."

"That would help," Paige agreed as she took her first good look at Cozumel. "Oh, my, this is beautiful. The beach is so clean and white." She was used to the beaches in Miami, which weren't nearly as pristine and inviting.

"I hear the snorkeling is spectacular. Ever been?"

Paige shook her head. "I don't like to swim in the ocean—I'm not a strong swimmer."

"You don't have to be. We can rent some equipment, and I'll teach you. You'll love it, I promise."

"Love what?" Aurora asked with a mischievous smile, having caught the last bit of their conversation.

"Snorkeling," Paige supplied.

"Oh, good, I'm ready to hit the beach," Aurora said.

Paige was buoyed along by everyone else's enthusiasm, and soon she'd changed into her swimsuit, coated herself in sunscreen, and was wading out into the cool water wearing flippers and a mask and snorkel. Doc and Aurora had chosen to remain on shore, cozily ensconced under an umbrella and sipping frozen margaritas.

Paige soon forgot her apprehension about swimming in the ocean as she entered a world of colorful tropical fish and exotic coral formations. The salt water kept her afloat with no effort, and an hour passed quickly as she and Harrison paddled around, pointing out interesting specimens to each other. Paige thought the most interesting specimen in the sea, however, was her companion. More than once he caught her staring at him through her mask, watching him cut gracefully through the water, his body lean and tan, his muscles working smoothly.

After an exquisite lunch of fresh seafood at an outdoor café, where colorful, uncaged parrots watched the diners from perches, the foursome headed for the marketplace.

Paige had never been much of a shopper, but she amused herself by watching her mother ooh and aah over the tacky tourist merchandise. Aurora bought a leather wallet, a colorful bandana to add to her endless collection of scarves and the ugliest carved wooden marionette Paige had ever seen.

When they came to the jewelry merchants, Aurora was in her element. She tried on every outlandishly garish piece she could find, most of them wildly outside her budget.

Paige finally found something that interested her— a delicate, gold filigree necklace, as fine as a spider's web. She held it up to her neck and admired it in a mirror, aware that Harrison was watching her every move and obviously enjoying himself.

She reached for her wallet, but Harrison beat her to it. "I'll buy it for you."

"No, Harrison, you don't have to—"

"I want to," he said, handing the merchant a wad of Mexican money.

"But it's not—"

"I don't expect anything in return," he said, his meaning clear. "I just want to give you a little something, okay? You didn't even let me buy you lunch."

"Oh, for heaven's sake, Paige," Aurora interjected. "It's a twenty-dollar necklace. Let the man buy it."

Outnumbered and overruled, Paige gave in. Harrison fastened the necklace around her neck, his fingers brushing against her skin as he worked the tiny clasp. She wore it the rest of the day, reaching up often to touch it, admiring it in every store window she passed.

She was nuts, she told herself more than once. The fact that he'd wanted to give her a gift pleased her no end, although it probably meant little to him. She'd wanted some distance from Harrison, and all she was doing was getting herself in deeper.

As for preventing her mother from committing marriage number five, Paige wasn't optimistic. Aurora and Doc were snug as two snails in the same shell. She tried to tell herself it wasn't such a bad thing. A retired doctor could at least support Aurora in style, and the two of them did seem compatible. But the thought of Bobby removing himself permanently from Aurora's life made Paige feel bleak inside.

Harrison couldn't take his eyes off the gold necklace. Or, more accurately, he couldn't stop looking at the pendant that dangled invitingly close to the shadow between Paige's breasts. He wanted Paige so desperately...but he knew he couldn't have her. It was bad enough that he was courting her. To actually take her to bed, then betray her by having her mother arrested, was just too low.

There was no question in his mind now that Aurora was their thief. When she had shown interest in Thelma Janks's emerald ring, Harrison's instincts had kicked in. This was his chance to catch Aurora in the act. After a quick consultation with James, during which he'd discovered the Janks's cabin was only three down from Aurora's, Harrison had stationed himself on the deck below Aurora's veranda and kept an eagle eye out for any nocturnal activities.

Unfortunately, Aurora had apparently changed her MO. The ring had disappeared, all right, along with a fourteen-karat gold money clip. But when James had investigated the theft early this morning, it appeared that the cat burglar had eschewed the balcony and glass door, and instead had somehow gotten past the magnetic security lock on the cabin door. Dan and Thelma had discovered the theft after breakfast this morning.

As he idly kicked up dust in the marketplace, Harrison's thoughts returned to Paige. He probably shouldn't have bought Paige the necklace, but he hadn't been able to resist. He'd wanted to give her something to remember him by. But the whole idea was dumb, he realized. Any pleasant memories she might harbor would be overridden by bitterness once she learned of his true identity. He would be lucky if she didn't drop the necklace overboard.

As the party of four continued to walk the market-place, Harrison formulated a plan of action that would get him inside Paige's cabin—tonight. He would have to get Doc's cooperation, and do it with-out alerting the older man that the object of his affec-tions was under suspicion. But he had an idea for that, too.

"So, Doc, seems like you and Aurora are getting along pretty well," Harrison observed, when the two ladies were busy trying on colorful straw hats.

"Ah, she's a fine woman," Doc responded, smil-ing fondly.

"Do you have big plans for the evening?" Harri-son waggled his eyebrows suggestively. "A bit of champagne and caviar in the privacy of your cabin, perhaps?"

"Well, now, that's certainly something to think about," Doc said. "Aurora could tempt a man in his grave. But I lost my dear Dotty only a couple of years ago, and I'm not sure I'm ready for anything so, er, adventurous. Female companionship is one thing—I'm sure Dotty wouldn't begrudge me that. But to actually partake in, well . . . how do I put it?"

"I know exactly what you mean," Harrison said reassuringly to the older man. "And I wasn't suggesting any impropriety. I just thought somewhere quiet, away from the crowds, you and Aurora could talk—really talk—and get to know each other better." And Paige would kill him if she knew the direction in which he was nudging Doc.

"I must say, we could use some time alone. Don't get me wrong, Aurora's niece is a wonderful girl, but she tends to hover over Aurora like a mother hen. And I imagine you'd like some time alone with the girl as well." Doc surveyed Harrison with a shrewd eye. "Ah, now I see what this is all about. You'd like me to keep the aunt occupied so the niece can concentrate on you."

Harrison nodded, flashing an embarrassed smile. "The thought had crossed my mind."

Doc winked conspiratorially. "I'll do my best to help you out. Say, now, I assume your intentions are honorable?"

"Strictly," Harrison said, inwardly wincing. He hated lying, especially to a nice old guy like Doc Waller. "You know, Paige is worried that you and Aurora might be hearing wedding bells. Not that she objects to you in particular. It's just that her aunt. . ."

"Yes, I'm aware of Aurora's marital track record. And Paige can rest assured I have no intentions in that direction. No one could ever replace my Dotty."

Well, at least Harrison could calm Paige's fears about her mother and husband number five. That would be small consolation, though, when Aurora was dragged off to jail.

The rest of the afternoon passed uneventfully. Paige and Harrison found a spot above deck on the tender boat for the return trip to the *Caribbean Mermaid,* and this time she suffered no ill effects.

"I talked to Doc," Harrison told her just before they pulled up next to the huge cruise ship. "Marriage is the furthest thing from his mind, as is seduction. He's still devoted to his wife. All he's seeking from Aurora is a little female companionship. So you can stop worrying."

"Oh, Harrison, that's wonderful! Thank you for talking to Doc. I'm sure it wasn't easy, bringing up such a sensitive subject." She smiled impishly. "Maybe you should have been a detective instead of a financial wheeler-dealer." Impulsively she stood on tiptoe and gave him what would have been a smack on the cheek—if Harrison hadn't turned his head at the last moment so that their lips collided.

The kiss was short but sweet. He knew Paige was uncomfortable with public displays of affection, and he forced himself to pull away after a few brief seconds of bliss. But even that small contact short-circuited his brain.

He struggled to bring his priorities firmly into line. "Have dinner with me?" he asked. Since they'd dined together every night so far, he didn't anticipate her rejection.

She shook her head. "I'm sorry. Mother wants to have dinner in our cabin tonight. She's wiped out and I'm pretty tired myself. But maybe...dessert? I heard something about a chocolate buffet on the Horizon Deck after dinner."

Harrison nodded enthusiastically. A bit of late-night sweets, a leisurely stroll back to her cabin, and with a little luck Paige would ask him inside. But that would do him no good if Aurora was there. If Doc didn't come through with an invitation, he had to think of a way to persuade Paige's mother to leave her cabin for a while.

That might take some doing. Even if Aurora did go out that night, he would have to coordinate things with James and make sure someone was watching her while Harrison was alone with Paige. He had already blown his surveillance of Aurora twice. Any more foul-ups, any more unwitnessed thefts, and he could kiss this assignment—not to mention his job—goodbye.

Oddly the prospect didn't bother him that much. The thought of kissing Paige goodbye bothered him a lot more. He'd sworn to never again allow his feelings to influence his work. Yet when it came right down to it, he was as much a victim of runaway emotion as Aurora Cheevers.

That thought was sobering. The role of victim did not suit him. He'd been there before and didn't like it.

Dammit, he wasn't going to repeat the same mistake he'd made with Kitty Cirello. Courting Paige, flirting with her, that was one thing. But he was feeling a lot more than professional interest in her. Well, no more! Starting now, tonight, he was taking back control of this case and himself.

* * *

Paige swirled the chocolate mousse around her tongue, savoring the bittersweet tingle. She had already indulged in chocolate-covered strawberries, angel cake dipped in chocolate fondue, and chocolate-raspberry cheesecake. She would have to take aerobics classes all day tomorrow to make up for these sins, and she had no one but herself to blame. The chocolate buffet had been her idea, one she now fervently wished she'd kept to herself.

Aurora, dressed in a muu-muu and with a gel mask over her face, had practically pushed Paige out the cabin door, insisting she keep her date with Harrison. "I'm fine, so don't worry about me," she'd said. "I just got a bit too much sun. I'll be perfectly all right by tomorrow."

Knowing Aurora was safely in bed—alone—had been tremendously liberating. Paige had made her way down to the Horizon Deck, more excited about seeing Harrison than she cared to admit. At last they would be alone.

It was extremely windy on deck. A sign informed Paige that, because of possible inclement weather, the chocolate bar had been moved indoors to a small dining area called the Gazebo. As soon as she came through the door she saw Harrison waiting for her. She offered him a bright smile, which he barely returned.

That was the moment she knew something was wrong. Harrison was polite but distant. He barely touched the chocolate delicacies he'd served himself, while Paige, suddenly nervous, had devoured hers.

What had happened between that hot, impulsive kiss on the deck of the tender boat and the tepid responses he was giving her now?

Moody SOB, she wanted to say. Was he one of these guys who enjoyed manipulating women's emotions? When they'd first met, and she'd staunchly refused to be charmed by him, had she unknowingly set up an irresistible challenge? And now that she was starting to really like him—more than like him, she admitted—was he losing interest?

"Mmm, you should try these brownies," Harrison said.

Paige pushed her plate away. "I can't eat another bite, or you'd have to roll me out of here. I've consumed enough chocolate to last me a year," she said glumly.

"Coffee, then?"

"That sounds good, but we better make it decaf." She started to rise when a sudden lurch of the ship sent her tumbling back into her chair. "Heavens, what was that?"

"A wave, I imagine," he said. "I heard we might be heading into stormy weather."

"Terrific." Thus far, the *Caribbean Mermaid*'s motion had been so subtle Paige had hardly been aware of it. Now suddenly she realized the ship was rocking decidedly to and fro. She could see the level of water in her glass slanting first one way, then the other.

"Stay put," Harrison said. "I'll get us both some coffee. You take yours black, right?"

She nodded distractedly, then started digging in her purse for motion sickness pills, which she hadn't taken all day. They weren't there. She'd left them in the cabin.

"Oh, great," she muttered.

"Something wrong?" Harrison set a cup of steaming coffee in front of her—some exotic, chocolate-flavored brew, judging from the smell. And the smell just about did her in.

"I, uh, just got suddenly tired," she said, improvising, keeping her voice steady, unemotional. "I think I'll go back to my cabin now. It's been . . . a nice evening, thanks." But when she stood, she found her knees were as substantial as pudding. The ship made another lurch, and she would have ended up on the floor if Harrison had not darted out of his chair and caught her.

"Paige?" he said, his voice full of concern.

When she looked up into his eyes she saw not the cold, distant man who'd been sitting across from her moments earlier, but the warm, caring man she'd come to know this afternoon. His quicksilver moods were confusing her, but right now that was a secondary consideration.

First, she had to get back to her cabin. She was going to be violently ill.

Six

"Let's get you back to your cabin," Harrison said, brushing a strand of hair from her damp forehead. "Can you walk?"

"I . . . I think so."

"Never mind." Before she could even offer a protest, he put one arm around her shoulders, the other behind her knees, and swung her up in his arms, unheedful of the curious stares they were drawing. He managed to grab her evening bag off the table before heading out of the Gazebo. "Why didn't you tell me you weren't feeling well?"

"Honestly, until a few seconds ago I was fine," she said miserably. "It hit me like a grand piano falling out of the sky, and will you put me down? I can walk."

"You're weak as a kitten. I can feel you trembling. So just hush and let me take care of you. Seasick," he added, obviously explaining the situation to some curious onlooker.

"I'm so embarrassed," Paige mumbled, her face hidden against his firm shoulder. "I'll never be able to face these people again...." But then another wave of nausea hit her, and she didn't care what anyone thought. She just wanted to make it to her cabin and suffer in peace.

This was just perfect, she thought, thoroughly annoyed with herself. Of all the times for her motion sickness to hit, why now? Why, when she was with Harrison? He would be so impressed when she threw up on him.

"Could we find a door and go out for fresh air?" she said in a thready voice.

"It's pouring down rain outside," Harrison replied, his voice soothing. "Take some deep breaths. That's it. We'll be at your cabin soon."

Paige was vaguely aware that they'd gotten onto the elevator.

"Seasick," Harrison said again to whoever was on the elevator with them.

Paige moaned. Why couldn't she just die right here?

When they arrived at the door to her cabin, Harrison set her down on shaky legs and searched her purse for the room key.

"I'll find it," she protested feebly, but he'd already pulled the magnetic card out of the bag. She stood aside and let him open the door, unwilling to battle with the balky electronic lock tonight.

The moment the door clicked open, she breathed a small sigh of relief. She wasn't going to completely humiliate herself. "Thank you, Harrison, for seeing me back to my—" she started, but he pushed the door open and guided her inside, then shut it behind them. "Wait, you can't stay," she objected. "I didn't ask you in."

He smiled indulgently. "You expect me to run off and leave you when you're at death's door?"

She didn't have time to stand there and argue. The ship lurched again, along with her stomach, and she bolted for the bathroom, slamming the door.

The next few minutes weren't pretty, made more miserable still by the fact that Paige couldn't think of anything except Harrison on the other side of that thin door, hearing every move she made. Please, if there is a God, make Harrison go away. She didn't want him to see her like this.

Harrison paced the small cabin, feeling guilty as hell. He shouldn't have encouraged her to eat all that chocolate, no matter how much she appeared to be enjoying it. Knowing they were headed into rough seas, he should have reminded her to take her medicine. He should have done something—should be doing something now. He felt utterly helpless.

The worst thing was, she didn't want him here.

He knocked tentatively on the door. "Paige? You okay? Do you want me to call the ship's doctor, or Doc Waller?"

She opened the door a crack and peered out with one eye. "I'm fine, honestly. Please go away."

"Why? You're sick. Someone needs to take care of you. Where are your motion sickness pills, anyway?"

"I think they're in Mother's cabin. I . . ." Suddenly she clamped her eyes shut. "Oh, Lord." She shut the door in Harrison's face.

Harrison had to find those pills before this got any worse. He hated to wake Aurora, considering what happened the last time he'd disturbed her sleep, but he had no choice. He went to the connecting door and raised his fist to knock. But before he could do it, the door opened, revealing a surprised Aurora—dressed to the nines in a glittery top, spandex pants and spike heels. She was enveloped in a cloud of very strong perfume.

"Oh, excuse me, Harrison, I didn't realize you were here." She scanned the room over his shoulder. "Where's Paige?"

"Bathroom. Seasick. I was just coming to ask you if you had those pills she takes. Are you going out?"

"I took a nap and got my second wind, so I was planning to check out the disco," she said, giving her hips a little shake as she turned toward her own cabin. "Let's see, the pills are...right here, on my dresser. Is she terribly sick?"

"Pretty sick," Harrison said, looking casually around Aurora's cabin. Here he was, right where he'd been trying to get for the past three days. He didn't see anything incriminating. But what had he expected, that she would leave the stolen jewelry lying around?

Aurora picked up the bottle of pills. "I guess I can do the disco some other night. Can't very well leave Paige here alone if she's sick."

"She won't be alone," Harrison hastened to explain. "I'll stay with her."

"Oh, but you don't need to—"

"I don't mind, honestly. You don't want to disappoint Doc Waller, do you?"

She waved her hand dismissively. "Oh, he's being an old fuddy-duddy tonight. Too pooped to pop, he said."

FREE

Return this card, and we'll send you four specially selected Silhouette Desires absolutely FREE! We'll even pay the postage and packing for you!

We're making this offer to introduce you to the benefits of Reader Service: FREE home delivery of brand-new romances at least a month before they're available in the shops, a FREE gift and a monthly Newsletter packed with information.

Accepting these FREE books places you under no obligation to buy, you may cancel at any time simply by writing to us — even after receiving just your free shipment.

Yes, please send me four free Silhouette Desires, and a mystery gift. I understand that unless you hear from me, I will receive six superb new titles every month for just £2.20* each postage and packing free. I am under no obligation to purchase any books and I may cancel or suspend my subscription at any time, but the free books and gifts will be mine to keep in any case.

(I am over 18 years of age).

1S6SD

Ms/Mrs/Miss/Mr _____

Address _____

_____

_____ Postcode _____

*Prices subject to change without notice.

Silhouette Reader Service

FREEPOST
Croydon
Surrey
CR9 3WZ

Offer closes 30th June 1996. We reserve the right to refuse an application. *Prices and
terms subject to change without notice. Offer valid in U.K. and Ireland only and is not available
to current subscribers of this series. Overseas readers please write for details. Southern
Africa write to: IBS Private Bag X3010, Randburg 2125.

You may be mailed with offers from other reputable companies as a result of this application.
If you would prefer not to share in this opportunity, please tick box. ☐

"Well, I'm sure you won't lack for dance partners."

She smiled and preened a bit. "Thank you, Harrison. If you're sure you don't mind. . . . Paige can get a little out of sorts when she's not feeling well. Promise you won't hold it against her?"

"I won't, I promise."

"In that case—I won't stay out late." With that she gave herself a final spritz of perfume and breezed out the door.

This was perfect, Harrison thought. He could stay with Paige until she fell asleep, then return to Aurora's cabin through the connecting door and give the place a thorough search. If Paige or Aurora caught him, he could claim he was looking for something—like stomach medicine, or maybe an ice pack.

It was a terrible thing to take advantage of Paige's illness, but when else would he get a chance like this?

He returned to the bathroom door and knocked again. When she opened it a crack, he handed her the bottle of pills. "Thanks," she said, then retreated.

While Paige was occupied, Harrison took the opportunity to call James and tell him that Aurora was on the loose.

"You mean I have to go traipsing up to the disco at this hour?" James complained.

"If that's where she really went," Harrison said. "I can't follow her. I'm in Paige's cabin, and this might be the only chance I have to search the place."

"So, you're in, huh?" James's sounded suddenly interested. "You gonna score?"

Harrison gritted his teeth. "None of your business," he said, before slamming down the phone.

Paige finally emerged about fifteen minutes later, her face scrubbed clean and slightly pink from the day's sun, her hair pulled back from her face. She was wearing a thin cotton robe and very little else, from what Harrison could tell. She looked sexy as hell.

Harrison chastised himself for even thinking along those lines. Paige needed TLC right now, not lust.

She smiled weakly. "I think I'm going to live," she said, "although I wouldn't have thought so a few minutes ago. Was my mother upset that you woke her?"

"I didn't wake her. She was on her way out the door, off to the disco."

Paige's face fell. "Oh, no."

"Don't worry, I called James and asked him to keep an eye on her."

"You didn't tell him—"

"No," he quickly reassured Paige. "I just told him you were worried about her gallavanting alone on the ship, and he said he'd make sure she arrived safely back at her cabin." That wasn't exactly the truth, Harrison thought, but it was close.

"Well, I guess he's better than a stranger. But I've come to the conclusion that Mother's going to do what she wants no matter what I say. Thanks for looking out for her, though."

"No charge." He walked over to where Paige was standing, not quite sure what he was going to do. When he reached her, he put a hand to her forehead. "No fever."

"You don't get fever with seasickness, silly."

"I was afraid it might be something else. You had me worried."

"I'll be fine. A good night's sleep, and by morning I'll be right as rain. Uh, you can go now."

He took her hand and led her to the bed, then pulled the covers back. "I'm not going anywhere. I'm staying until I'm sure you're okay."

He expected her to argue, but instead she gave a resigned smile and a shrug. "I'm not going to talk you out of this, am I?"

He shook his head.

"Gee, what an interesting date I've been. First you get to watch me pig out on chocolate, then I get sick, and now you get the privilege of watching me fall asleep. I'll probably drool." She yawned elaborately.

"This has been the most . . . eventful date I've had in quite a while." He gave her a chaste kiss on the forehead. "Don't you want to take off your robe?"

The look she gave him was full of suspicion. "I may be slightly debilitated at the moment, but I'm not stupid." With that she climbed into the bed and pulled the blankets up to her chin.

Harrison laughed. "It was worth a try." He turned off the light, then sat on the edge of the bed and took off his shoes. "Scoot over."

"I beg your pardon? You're not getting—"

"I'm going to get comfortable. On top of the covers. Fully clothed. Paige, only a mindless jerk would try to take advantage of a situation like this."

"That's what I'm worried about," she said with a touch of her old antagonism. But she did scoot over and let him lie down next to her, proving that she really did believe him.

After several moments of quiet Paige giggled.

"What's so funny."

"It's just that I never visualized going to bed with you quite like this."

"Ah-ha, but you have visualized going to bed with me?"

"Well, I mean . . . haven't you?" she countered.

"Too many times, and in too many ways, to count. But never like this, you're right. Lift up your head." When she complied, he put his arm around her, pillowing her head on his shoulder. "Good night, Paige. Sweet dreams."

Although the contact between them was fairly innocent, Paige's nearness, the heat and scent of her, would likely drive Harrison wild in record time. He wanted to touch her, to pull those covers off and find out what she was wearing under that robe. But he'd already said it—only a real jerk would take advantage of a sick woman, no matter how tempting she was.

In less than five minutes Paige was asleep. He could tell by the deep, regular breathing, the total relaxation of her body. This was the perfect opportunity. Aurora probably wouldn't be back for hours, and Paige wasn't likely to awaken when she was drugged up on seasickness pills.

He sat up gingerly, listening for any change in Paige's breathing. She slept on in blissful ignorance of the fact that her date was about to take advantage of the situation in ways she'd never imagined.

He started to stand, then stopped. He couldn't do it. Dammit, he simply couldn't do this to Paige. She had allowed him to lie next to her on the bed. She'd fallen asleep in his arms. She must really trust him. How could he possibly turn around and betray her hard-won faith?

He couldn't. He would have to confess to James that he'd turned soft. He would take himself off the case. Hell, he wouldn't have to. James would fire him, and then the agency Harrison worked for would fire him. He'd be unemployed. And when Paige found out who he was and what he'd been up to—and she would find out, because he was going to have to confess everything to her—he would lose her, too.

All because he'd let a beautiful woman get under his skin. Again.

But this was much different than the situation with Kitty, he reminded himself. Paige was innocent of any wrongdoing. She wasn't manipulating him for her own selfish purposes, as Kitty had done.

Well, he was only getting what he deserved, he figured. He should have listened to his instincts and turned down this job, no matter what kind of pressure his boss had put on him. He'd never enjoyed undercover work, and he should have stuck by his principles.

Harrison's thoughts chased each other around in endless circles until he fell into an uneasy sleep.

Paige woke up feeling one hundred percent better. Gone were all signs of nausea and weakness. In fact, she felt oddly snug and secure, even though she was fully aware of the ship's motion. Now, however, the rhythmic rocking felt more like a hammock or a cradle, instead of the nightmarish carnival ride it had seemed earlier.

A soft snoring in her ear quickly dispelled her sense of well-being. Harrison! What was he still doing here? What if her mother came in? Paige leaned up on one elbow, switched on the bedside lamp and looked at her watch. It was almost four in the morning.

She allowed herself to relax. If Aurora were going to pop in and say good-night, she would already have done so.

Paige was sure Harrison hadn't meant to fall asleep. But since he had, she took the opportunity to study him at leisure. He was the most handsome man she'd ever seen, much less shared a bed with. In his current rumpled state, with his hair mussed and his shirttail half out and his cheek shadowed with beard stubble, he seemed completely harmless.

How could she have ever thought those terrible things she'd accused him of? He might be a flirt, but as far as she could tell that was the worst of his faults. Any man who would stick around while his date threw up in the bathroom, then gently care for her as Harrison had, was a prince. A real, eighteen-karat prince.

"Harrison," she whispered.

He didn't bat an eyelash.

So, he was a sound sleeper? Hmm. Unable to resist, she leaned over and kissed him, first on his bristly cheek, then on his mouth.

His response was immediate and heated. He wrapped his arms more tightly around her body and opened his mouth against hers, kissing her like a dying man granted his last wish.

Paige knew the instant he came fully awake. His eyes popped open and his whole body stiffened.

She pulled back, smiling. "Good morning."

"What? How..."

"Didn't your mother ever tell you not to fall asleep in a strange girl's bed? She might ravish you."

He leaned up on his elbows, ran his hand over his face and looked down at his fully clothed body. At last comprehension dawned. "Paige, I'm sorry. I didn't mean to fall asleep. How do you feel?" Finally he smiled, and a decidedly devilish light shone in his eyes. "I guess you already answered that question. Feeling pretty perky, are we? Perky enough to kiss me awake?"

"You gave your word you wouldn't take advantage of the situation. I, however, never made such a promise."

"Ah, I see," he said thoughtfully, laying his head back on the pillow. "Now, if I were a truly honorable man, I would realize that with the seasickness and all, you've taken temporary leave of your senses. I would immediately get up and bid you a hasty good night. But..."

"But?"

"I'm not that honorable." He deftly rolled on top of her, the covers still between them, and pinned her arms above her head. "I'll teach you to play with fire."

She was laughing when he kissed her, but all humor fled as the kiss grew more insistent, filling her with a warm lethargy. She'd known she was playing with fire. She fully expected to get singed.

Paige sighed as he trailed warm, wet kisses across her cheek and under her ear. He released her hands, and she wrapped them around his neck, burying her fingers in his thick, soft hair. Even through clothing and layers of blankets she could feel the strength of his desire for her. This was no longer a game. They were perilously close to crossing the line, here. The mere thought sent a poignant longing through her whole body.

"Paige?" he whispered, inching the covers down so he could kiss her collarbone. "Are you sure you're up to this?"

"Mmm, I'm more than up for it. I feel . . . terrific. Better all the time." Better than she had in her whole life. She couldn't stand all this fabric between them. She wanted to feel him down the whole length of her body, flesh to flesh. She wanted to take off this dumb, unsexy cotton robe and toss the blankets on the floor. Then she wanted to undress Harrison, button by button.

Fueled by her wanton thoughts, her hands sought out the front of his shirt, and she began to unfasten it.

"Paige?"

"Hmm?"

"Is this what you really want?"

"Would I be trying to strip you if it wasn't?" When he didn't smile, her own brief amusement faded. "Harrison, of course it's what I want. I don't take this lightly. I know we're just two people who met up on a ship, and we probably won't see each other when the cruise is over, but I want this just the same. I've thought about it. I want you."

He tenderly caressed her face. "I hope so. Because I couldn't stand it if you regretted this—"

She silenced him with a quick kiss, then gazed deeply into his eyes, wanting to make him understand. "No regrets, I promise."

He kissed her back, and the flames flared between them again. Paige resumed working on the shirt buttons, fumbling in her haste. When she had the shirt half-open, she slid her hands inside and pressed them against his chest, the springy curls tickling her palms.

"Paige?"

"What?" she asked, stifling her impatience. The man had set her on fire, and he was going to talk her to death.

"What are we going to do about protection?"

She fell back against the pillow, ashamed of herself. Protection had been the farthest thing from her mind. "I'd forgotten," she admitted. "But fortunately, my mother has adopted the Boy Scout motto for her own, and she looks out for me. Check the drawer in the bedside table."

He had to roll off her to reach the drawer, and she took the opportunity to yank the covers aside.

"Ah-hah," he said, holding up a foil packet. "Bless you, Aurora."

"Now, if we're done chatting," Paige said, crooking her finger at him.

He smiled indulgently as he finished the job she'd started on his shirt, then tossed it aside. "I have just one more question. What do you have on under that prim little robe?"

She smiled wickedly. "Why do you think I wouldn't take it off last night? I'm not wearing anything underneath."

He groaned and pulled her to him, and this time there were no more words between them. Harrison inched the hem of her robe up her thigh, then slid his hand beneath it, cupping her bottom. The sudden, intimate contact took her breath away. She heard a low moan and realized it was hers.

He kneaded her hip with one hand and opened her robe with the other, baring her breasts. They were full and firm and milky white, and she'd always considered them too large. But the way Harrison looked at them, she knew he liked them, and the realization filled her with a warm pleasure.

He brought both hands up to touch them, circling the sensitive nipples with trembling fingers, then cupping them fully in his palms, and finally pressing a kiss to each one.

Paige had never felt more beautiful, more desirable. She threw her head back, exposing her throat. Harrison kissed her there, too, as he slid her robe off her shoulders and down. She dispensed with it, glad to be rid of it. Between them, working with fevered hands, they peeled Harrison out of the rest of his clothes until they were both lying blissfully naked on the bare sheet, fully illuminated by the lamp, unashamed.

"I could look at you all night," he said, his voice thick with emotion.

"I hope you'll do more than look."

"Oh, I intend to." He reached out and laid his hand flat against her belly, causing her to take a sharp breath. Slowly he inched his way downward, feverishly exploring the dark red curls that guarded her womanhood, stroking her inner thighs, making her ache for completion.

"Where's that little packet?" she murmured, the words emerging dreamlike. Her mind had dropped its control; her body was in the lead now.

Harrison quickly took care of necessities, but he didn't rush Paige. He slowly, deliberately kissed her again, still stroking her, encouraging her to make her own tentative explorations of his body.

Although Paige wasn't terribly experienced, she'd thought she knew what went where. But she'd had no idea lovemaking could be like this, so soft and sweet and gentle. While she'd enjoyed intimacy with Curtis, he'd never taken the time to please her as thoroughly as Harrison was doing, to build up the tension between them until she thought she might burst from sheer excitement.

With insistent tugs and nudges, she tried to urge him to lie atop her. But he surprised her by pulling her on top of him. "You started this seduction, remember?" he said in a husky voice. "That means you get to call the shots. It's your show."

Paige didn't want to admit she'd never done it like this before. So with more enthusiasm than expertise, she slowly lowered herself onto Harrison's body, feeling him gradually fill her. Then she rose up on her knees and did it again. And again.

The sensations were incredible. She couldn't have believed anything would feel so wondrous, so emotionally satisfying. Softness and gentleness were replaced with high intensity as she rode him hard, drawing him deeply inside her. She closed her eyes and let her instincts guide her, feeling like she'd reached some otherworldly horizon as their bodies and spirits became one.

Just when she thought they might float away on some orgasmic cloud, it was over in one giant, cataclysmic earthquake of pure sensation. The next thing she remembered she was slumped over on top of him, slick with perspiration and breathing like she'd run a marathon.

"Are you okay, sweetheart?" he whispered, smoothing her hair out of her face.

"Better than okay," she said between gasps, still full of wonder. "You?"

He gave a throaty laugh. "What do you think?"

"Truthfully? I have no idea. I was in my own little world."

"I was there with you, sweetheart." He pulled her to him and kissed her so tenderly she thought her heart would melt. How was she ever going to give him up when the cruise was over?

Harrison lay awake long after Paige had drifted off. Making love with her had been nothing short of incredible. He wished he could stay here indefinitely, with her curled up next to him, her head resting trustingly against his chest. They were safe and secure in the cocoon of intimacy they'd created.

But it couldn't last. He needed to get out of here before daylight...before Aurora found him here like this. It was one thing to espouse a liberal attitude about sex; it was another to actually discover your darling daughter in bed with a man she'd met less than three days ago.

But his melancholy went further than that. He had a rocky road ahead of him, some difficult confessions to make. The next few hours would cause some drastic changes in his life. James would have a coronary. Harrison's boss would go ballistic.

And Paige...well, it was a cinch Paige wouldn't forgive easily, if at all, no matter how he explained things. She was not a woman who gave her trust lightly. Once betrayed, she would never trust him again.

The sky was starting to grow light. As gently as he could, Harrison extricated himself from Paige's cozy embrace. She stirred, and her eyes fluttered open. "Where ya going?" she asked muzzily.

"I have to go back to my own cabin," he answered, his voice tinged with regret. "Maybe I'm a little old-fashioned, but I'd prefer it if the whole world doesn't know I spent the night with you."

"Aw, who cares," she said with a low laugh.

"You do, and you know it. Imagine what your mother would think."

"She'd applaud." Paige closed her eyes. "Oh, all right, you can leave. I refuse to be one of those clingy, whiny, insecure women. Just because you're slithering away in the middle of the night—"

"It's not the middle of the night. It's after six."

"Oh."

Harrison somehow managed to find his clothes in the darkness and climb into them. Then he sat on the edge of the bed and took her hands in his. "Would it be really trite for me to say you were wonderful? That the whole thing was . . . incredible, beyond my wildest dreams?"

"Mmm, yeah, but go ahead. I love a good lie, if it's told for the right reasons."

Her words pricked his conscience. "You know it's not a lie," he said, leaning down to kiss her. "I'll see you around lunchtime, okay?"

"Okay," she said drowsily. "Thanks, Harrison."

"For what?"

"That was the best bout of seasickness I ever had."

He tucked the covers around her the way he might for a precious child, then turned to leave. If he didn't walk away from her now, he never would.

In his haste he brushed too close to the dresser and knocked something onto the floor—a scarf, along with something jangly. Curious, he leaned over and picked up the jangly thing. It was a necklace of some sort.

With apprehension building in his gut, he carried the item over to the veranda door, where the light of dawn crept in, illuminating the trinket in his hand. The dazzling stones winked knowingly at him, seeming to mock him.

Harrison didn't want to believe his eyes. But there could be no mistaking this particular necklace. He'd seen the sketch the owner had made and then had listened to a detailed description. He was holding the stolen sapphire-and-diamond necklace.

He felt like he'd been kicked in the gut. In an instant all the tender feelings he'd harbored for Paige turned to ashes.

Seven

When Paige woke up several hours later, her first thought was that last night must have been a dream. But then she pressed her face against the pillow Harrison had lain on, and it still carried his scent. She hugged the pillow to her. Maybe cruise ships weren't so bad after all.

She got up, filled with energy and optimism. After choosing something to wear, she was thinking about a shower, when her mother knocked on the connecting door—something she seldom did. Aurora usually barged right in.

"Come in," Paige called.

Aurora inched the door open and peeked inside. "Is the coast clear?"

"What are you talking about?" Paige replied a tad too defensively.

"Harrison. Is he gone?"

"Well of course he's gone. It's—" Paige looked at her watch "—nine in the morning. What would he be doing here? For that matter, what are you doing up at the crack of dawn?" she asked, hoping to divert her mother's attention from the subject of Harrison.

"I came in early last night," she explained, automatically smoothing the covers up on the bed and fluffing the pillows. "I went to the disco, but it wasn't much fun. James was there, hanging around like a puppy waiting for a table scrap. No one was going to ask me to dance while he was there, so I came back. Besides, I was worried about you. How are you feeling this morning? As if I had to ask," she added with a low chuckle.

Oh, great. With that mother's sixth sense of hers, Aurora knew exactly what had gone on here last night.

"I'm feeling much better," Paige answered as casually as she could.

"I imagine you are." Aurora idly opened the drawer on the bedside table, then closed it again. "Mmm-hmm."

Ordinarily Paige would have been put out at her mother's prying, but she just couldn't find it in her heart this morning to be angry at anyone. "All right, all right, I slept with him. Are you satisfied?"

Aurora grinned like a Cheshire cat. "I'm delighted! The question is, are you satisfied?"

Paige couldn't help smiling, too, despite the fact that she knew her face was turning red. "It was unbelievable."

"I knew it would be. See, you've got more of your mother in you than you thought. And you always make fun of my shipboard romances. I'm telling you, it's the sea air."

That sobered Paige. Heavens, she was behaving just like her mother.

"I hope you and Harrison are making plans for when the cruise is over," Aurora said.

"No," Paige answered sharply. "That's where you and I differ. I'll agree that a shipboard fling can be terrific. But the cruise is…a fantasyland. It would be silly of me to expect a relationship with Harrison to continue once we're back in the real world." But wasn't that exactly what she'd been thinking? Maybe not consciously, but in the back of her mind she had already entertained thoughts about her and Harrison and a white picket fence. She couldn't deny it.

"I've taken mine back to the real world," Aurora said.

"But they didn't last," Paige pointed out.

Aurora's voice went dreamy. "Some of them did, for a while."

"I don't want just 'a while,'" Paige said, sinking to the bed. "I want forever."

"So? Marry the guy. You'll never know if it will last forever unless you try."

"Marry him? Like he's mine for the asking, just like that?" But suddenly Paige saw the humor in the situation and chuckled. "Wouldn't Daddy have a fit over that? I'm supposed to be keeping you from getting married, not going off and getting married my—" Paige clamped her hand over her mouth. Oh, good heavens, she'd really done it this time. Her father would kill her. After Aurora did.

Aurora's eyebrows flew up. "You're supposed to be keeping me from getting married? And just whose idea was this?" She spoke through gritted teeth. "That rat. He has no right—"

"Now, Mother, don't be angry. We were only looking out for you—"

"And so you and your father decided I needed a watchdog?" Aurora folded her arms and tapped her foot, clearly disgusted. "I should have known to be suspicious when you suddenly showed an interest in cruising with me."

"It was a crazy idea, I'll admit it. If you want to marry Doc Waller or Captain Barnes or the flamenco dancer, it's really none of my business. It's just that..."

"What?" Aurora snapped.

"Daddy said that if you got married again, he was washing his hands of you. He said he wouldn't bail you out again. And I just couldn't let him do that. You need Daddy."

Aurora put her hands on her hips. "Really, Paige! I need Bobby Stovall like I need a lobotomy. I'll admit, your father has been more than generous with me over the years. But I can certainly get along without him, if that's his attitude. You've always clung to this adolescent fantasy that your parents will get back together. But would you really like to see that? Don't you remember the arguments, the tears—"

"But you've both changed and grown so much since then," Paige said. "It was the money that did it, the sudden wealth after we'd been so poor for so long. By now you've both had a chance to adjust to that. And Daddy still loves you, I know that. He's always cared for you. Why do you think he never remarried?"

"Because he couldn't find another woman stupid enough?" Aurora suggested. But her fond smile took the sting out of the words. "Oh, for heaven's sake, what's done is done. No sense arguing further about it. Hurry up, get your shower, and then let's go eat. I'm starving.''

Paige slipped into the bathroom, relieved she'd gotten off so easily. Her mother could have blown a gasket over the scheme cooked up by her daughter and ex-husband, but she'd seemed only mildly miffed. Anyway, Paige had meant what she'd said about Aurora being free to marry whomever she chose. She might not agree with Aurora's choices, but the choices were not Paige's to make. She should have realized that sooner.

As for her own choices—dammit, she was not going to be like her mother, tripping in her haste to get to the altar just because a few hormones were running rampant. She was not going to end up like Aurora—pinning her hopes on the perfect man, only to be disappointed in the long run.

When this cruise was over, she and Harrison were finished, too. She had to face up to that fact.

"You look like hell," James said cheerfully as he dug into his plateful of eggs and bacon.

Harrison made a caveman sound in acknowledgment. He couldn't possibly look as bad as he felt. He'd gotten little sleep last night, and he'd barely managed to pull himself together this morning for his meeting with James. The only thing he could manage to choke down was scalding black coffee.

"So, why all the urgency? Did you find anything last night?"

Harrison hesitated for several moments. Part of him wanted to protect Paige and her mother, but he ruthlessly quashed those softer feelings. "Yeah. The sapphire necklace. It's in Paige's room.''

James stared for a moment in disbelief. Then a wide smile erupted on his face as he rubbed his hands together in obvious glee. "Hot damn! Paige's room, huh? Then she's in on it with her mother?"

"It appears that way."

"Huh. Never would have guessed that." James was suddenly all business. "Okay, we have to be extra careful now so they don't suspect we're onto them. If Aurora smells a rat, she'll dispose of the hidden jewelry and we'll never be able to pin a thing on her."

"How long before we can conduct the search?" Harrison asked.

"We'll have to go see the captain, present the evidence to him, and he'll authorize the search. He's the law, judge and jury while we're on the high seas."

"And how long will that take?" Harrison wanted this thing over as soon as possible.

"Well, the captain's a busy man. First he'll have to make time for us, and then I'm sure he'll want to think things over. He's not one to jump to rash action. But I'd say it'll all be resolved in twenty-four hours or less."

Twenty-four hours? That sounded like forever. "And once the search is over, and the evidence is recovered?"

"Again, it's up to the captain. He could confine them to their cabin. Or he could throw them into the brig."

Harrison wondered what the brig was like. He had a sudden, unpleasant vision of Paige and her mother in some dank rat hole in the bowels of the ship. Bread and water. Walking the plank.

"Personally," James continued glibly, "I'd be perfectly satisfied if he just tossed them off the ship in Grand Cayman—that's our next port of call. But I don't think they'll get away that easily."

"You mean they'll face criminal charges?" Harrison asked. "Where?"

James nodded. "It's not just the captain who wants to nail the thief. Mermaid Cruise Line's CEO is involved, too. He intends to recover the other jewelry stolen on previous cruises, or at least recover damages. If Mermaid decides to prosecute, the ladies will be transported to our country of registry."

"And that country is . . . ?"

"Liberia."

"Africa? They'd have to go to Africa?" Lord, no telling what kind of jails they had there. Or what kind of justice system. Harrison's stomach suddenly tied itself into a knot.

Dammit, he had to be tough about this. A thief was a thief, no matter how charming. Or sexy. Or soft and warm and smelling subtly of strawberries from the scented lotion she used. . . .

"So you'll have to play this game awhile longer," James was saying.

Harrison snapped back to the present. "What?"

"Until we can arrange for the search, you'll have to keep doing what you've been doing. Act perfectly normal."

The realization hit Harrison like a two-by-four to the head. He would have to see Paige, pretend nothing had changed, spend the day with her . . . and the night.

Could he do it? Could he make love to her again knowing what kind of woman she really was?

An unpleasant thought occurred to him. "James, you don't suppose the ladies are already on to me, do you?"

"How do you figure that?"

"Well, if you had stolen a twenty-seven-thousand-dollar necklace, wouldn't you take pains to hide it? Hide it really well? It seems they made it awfully easy for me to find it."

"But why would they do that?"

"I don't know...to make me look like an idiot? I mean, suppose even now they're hiding the stolen jewelry somewhere outside their cabins—in a potted plant, for instance, or in a locker at the health club. We accuse Aurora of being a thief, search their cabins and—"

"Nothing." James tapped his chin with his forefinger. "That would be ugly. Certainly would generate some damaging publicity, if not a lawsuit. But how could they have figured out who you are?"

Harrison racked his brain. There was no way. He hadn't slipped up anywhere.

"Maybe Aurora got scared, and she left the necklace in Paige's cabin to implicate her," James said.

Harrison shook his head. He couldn't see Aurora betraying her own daughter. Although they had their differences, Aurora and Paige loved each other. There was no mistaking the closeness between them. Besides, Paige would have noticed a stray diamond-and-sapphire necklace left lying about.

No, there was no getting around it. Aurora might be the main perpetrator, but Paige was in it up to her pretty neck. He thought back to how stridently she'd objected when he'd come into her cabin last night, and how hard she'd tried to get him to leave. No doubt she'd been nervous because she'd left the necklace in plain sight.

How could he have misjudged her so badly? How could he have thought her so thoroughly innocent?

Hell, he might as well face it—he was a lousy judge of character. He'd thought so after his experience with Kitty Cirello, but now he knew it for a fact.

The two men discussed a few more possible legal actions resulting from this case, none of them pleasant. Harrison began to wish he'd never heard of Mermaid Cruise Lines or James Blair.

"Well, I've got a little action going on the side that I need to attend to," James said, his gaze floating over Harrison's shoulder.

Harrison casually looked behind him. The chesty brunette he'd met at the welcome cocktail party was smiling toothily at James. Pretty, but not his type, Harrison thought with a grimace. James could have her.

"I'll talk with the captain, then I'll find you." James smiled, though not pleasantly. "And you really ought to go clean up or something if you want to keep your little red-headed love bunny turned on. You're a mess." He stood abruptly and departed.

Harrison rubbed his face, realizing he hadn't shaved. Probably hadn't combed his hair, either. He'd showered and changed clothes—he remembered that—but otherwise he was pretty unkempt. If Paige saw him like this, she would wonder what was wrong, and he couldn't afford to arouse her suspicions. He'd better do as James said and tidy himself up.

Paige stepped onto the elevator, then stared at the buttons in indecision. Did she really want to lie by the pool and read? She'd gotten enough sun yesterday to last her the rest of the cruise, and she was worried she might run into James, who always made her nervous. She could jog around the track, but she really didn't have that much energy.

Truthfully, she'd have preferred to sit on her own little balcony, look out at the sea and perhaps write some postcards to her father and her friends back home. But if she stayed in her cabin, it would look like she was waiting for Harrison to call. She didn't want to give him the impression that just because they'd gone to bed she would be at his beck and call for the rest of the cruise.

Aurora had wanted Paige to call Harrison and make definite plans for lunch. "He'll think you're indifferent if you just ignore him," she'd insisted.

"Mother, he'll think I'm desperate if I call him," Paige had said firmly. "Now that he's made his conquest, he might not be interested anymore. And I absolutely will not chase him."

Aurora had been utterly bewildered. "What's the fun if you don't chase him?"

Paige had grinned. "Maybe I want him to chase me."

During the whole conversation, Paige had acted as if it didn't matter to her one way or another. But it did. More than she wanted to admit. How had this happened? How had she let herself fall head over heels for some financial genius bazillionnaire who lived a thousand miles from her?

Harrison probably had a string of sophisticated girlfriends at home, women with names like Penelope Smythe-Worthington and Cynthia Snodgrass, who played tennis and drank martinis at the country club.

To him, Paige was just a convenience, a novelty, perhaps.

Well, if it didn't mean anything to him, then it wouldn't to her, either. When she saw him again she would just smile distantly as if—

The elevator doors opened onto the Lido Deck and Harrison was standing there, conjured right out of her imagination. Paige knew the silly grin on her face was anything but distant. "H-hi."

He avoided looking her squarely in the eye, which didn't bode well. "Hi, yourself."

They stood there a couple of seconds, awkwardly silent, until Paige realized he was holding the door so she could get off the elevator.

"Oh, I—"

"Were you heading for the pool?" he asked.

Thankfully, he'd interrupting whatever dumb thing she was about to stutter. She nodded, stepping past him.

"I'll meet you there in about an hour and we can have lunch together. All right?"

She nodded again, at a complete loss for words. How could she have been so wantonly intimate with the man last night, and this morning be incapable of voicing the simplest of pleasantries?

"All right, then, see you later," he stepped aboard the elevator and was gone.

He'd looked a bit rumpled, she thought as she made her way dazedly to the pool area. Not that it mattered. He was still so gorgeous it made her chest hurt. But that was the first time she'd ever seen him less than perfectly groomed. It wasn't just his clothes or his hair. Something had seemed wrong, somehow out of kilter. He had smiled at her, but the smile hadn't radiated its usual warmth. He'd appeared distracted.

Oh, for heaven's sake, why was she obsessing about it? He'd made definite plans to see her later. He wasn't going to dump her, as she'd secretly feared. They were both simply suffering from a bit of morning-after jitters. Once they spent a few minutes together, everything would be fine.

Vowing not to let the peculiar encounter worry her another minute, she found herself a deck chair and made another stab at Stephen King.

Later, everything was not fine as Paige had hoped it would be. Harrison met her at the pool, as promised, looking neatly pressed and perfectly groomed. He was polite, solicitous even. He carried his end of the conversation, laughed at her dumb jokes and even cracked a few of his own. After lunch they joined Aurora and Doc Waller for shuffleboard, a game that Aurora had, until recently, claimed was only fit for old fogies.

Paige couldn't put her finger on what, exactly, disturbed her about Harrison's behavior. But he still had that detached air about him, as if something was really bothering him. It was like he was holding something back from her.

Later that afternoon she suggested they take a walk around the deck, and he agreed. He put his arm around her waist, as any attentive lover would. Was it possible she was imagining things? Being paranoid?

No, no, no. Something was wrong with this picture, and she was determined to get it out in the open. She paused at the railing close to the bow of the ship, where the wind was brisk and the salt spray tingled against her face.

Taking a deep breath, she went for it. "Harrison, is something wrong?"

"Wrong? No. Why would you think that?" he answered, sounding distinctly defensive.

"I don't know. You just seem...different today, like maybe since we made love last night you feel obligated to hang around with me now."

"Paige—"

"No, let me finish," she said, realizing she was about to bare her soul by throwing into the open her every insecurity. But these things had to be said. She and Harrison had to clear the air. "Neither of us planned what happened last night. And, if you'd rather, we can forget about it."

He was shaking his head vehemently. "No way. I couldn't forget it in a million years."

"I know you think I'm not very sophisticated about these things," she continued, ignoring his objection. "And you're such a nice person that you wouldn't deliberately hurt me or take me for granted now that we've, uh, satisfied our curiosity—"

"Is that all it meant to you?" he demanded, suddenly fierce. For the first time that day he looked her squarely in the eye. "Just satisfying curiosity?"

"No, no," she said quickly. "I'm not making myself clear, I guess."

"Well, what the hell is it you're trying to say?"

"I'm trying to say that you don't have to feel obligated to me just because we spent the night together. I'm a big girl and I can..." She paused and swallowed the lump that was forming in her throat. "I can handle it if you want to cool things. I'm not expecting anything—''

He abruptly interrupted her speech by hauling her into his arms and kissing the daylights out of her. It wasn't a gentle kiss. He pinned her to him with arms that felt like steel restraints and forced her head back with the strength of his mouth against hers. Dazed by his sensual onslaught, she could still sense the furious emotions behind the kiss—and the rampant desire. Whatever he'd been holding back all day he was releasing now.

He ended the kiss as abruptly as he'd started it, wrenching his mouth from hers and staring down at her, a maelstrom of emotions reflected in eyes that had darkened to almost black. ''Does that feel like I want to cool things?''

Her eyes filled with tears, despite her best efforts to keep from getting upset. ''Why are you mad at me?'' she asked. ''What have I done?''

Harrison's heart gave a painful lurch, and all of the anger drained out of him. No matter what she'd done, she didn't deserve such treatment. A jail sentence, perhaps, but not his deliberate cruelty. He wrapped his arms around her again—gently, this time—and pulled her against his chest, resting his cheek against her hair.

''I'm sorry, Paige.'' More sorry than she would ever know. ''I didn't mean to come on so strong. I'm just a little confused, that's all. I wasn't counting on this happening.''

''That makes two of us,'' she said, her voice muffled against his shirt.

He hugged her closer, absorbing her warmth and that damnable strawberry scent. He'd wanted so badly to hate Paige for her dishonesty, but he couldn't. The

green-eyed pirate had stolen more than just jewels—
she'd taken a piece of his heart for her own.

"Do you want me to bow out?" he asked. It hadn't
occurred to him until now that she might be the one
with cold feet.

"No, of course not. I was just trying to give you a
graceful exit, if you needed one. I thought maybe I'd
been a lousy lover, and you were trying to figure a way
out of having to repeat the experience."

He actually laughed at that. "If you're a lousy
lover, I'm Captain Kirk and this is the *Starship Enter-
prise.*"

"Then . . ." Paige pulled out of his embrace so she
could look at him. "You're saying you want to keep
on like we've been doing for the rest of the cruise?"

He could almost smile at Paige's quest for reassurance if it weren't so tragic. Hell, yes, he'd like to spend
the rest of the cruise with her. He wished he really were
some innocent financier instead of a private investigator who was about to ruin her life. He wished he
could forget about sapphire necklaces and all the de-
ceit on both sides. But any promises he made would be
broken.

"How about we just take things as they come,
huh?" He caressed her cheek, wishing he could do
better. "And maybe we should both stop worrying so
much."

She nodded, though he could tell she was disappointed with his answer. "I guess any sort of relationship, once the cruise is over, would be out of the
question."

Ah, hell. He'd had no idea she was that serious
about him—that she'd been thinking in terms of the
future. What made it ten times worse was that, under

any other circumstances, his thoughts would be running along the same lines. He'd be thinking up ways they could see each other after the cruise. He'd be wondering whether she would get along with his family, whether she would like his dog.

He hadn't allowed himself the luxury of such unattainable fantasies, and he couldn't allow her to believe in the future, either. That would be the ultimate cruelty. "I don't see how," he said sadly. "We live a thousand miles apart."

"Right." She turned and leaned her elbows on the railing, staring out at the empty ocean.

"Paige..." He put his arms around her from behind and nuzzled her neck. "That doesn't mean we can't enjoy the here and now. Things have been so good. The last thing I want to do is spoil it."

"You haven't spoiled anything," she said. "I appreciate your honesty."

Honesty? he thought with self-loathing. He'd done nothing but lie to Paige since meeting her. The only honest thing about him was his increasing desire for her. That was real.

She was wearing a sea green T-shirt over matching shorts, and he slid his arm underneath it and around her midriff, reveling in the silky feel of her skin. His body shielded his actions from the view of any curious passersby. "I could make love to you right here, this very minute," he said, amazed at the sudden passion he felt.

Paige gave a throaty laugh. "Right here on deck? I think the captain might have something to say about that."

Harrison whirled her around to face him. "I'm serious. Come to my cabin with me." He wanted to lose himself in her, to forget everything except the feel of her body wrapped round his and the ecstasy of burying himself deep inside her. Only there, in that special communion they shared, could he escape from his own wretched thoughts.

Eight

"**A**ll right." Paige's voice trembled. She really felt wanton, agreeing to make love in the afternoon with a man who'd just told her in no uncertain terms that they had no future. He couldn't even commit to the next twenty-four hours, much less a month or a year or a lifetime.

But none of that seemed to matter at the moment. They had the here and now, as Harrison had pointed out, and she was powerless to say no to him.

She wanted him.

He'd created a powerful mental picture with his bold suggestion that they make love right there on the deck, and the sensual images stayed with her as they made their way hand in hand to the elevators.

They didn't say a word to each other, but the tension between them was so tangible that Paige suspected every person they passed knew what she and

Harrison had on their minds. She didn't really care. She was so crazy for Harrison Powell, she wanted the whole world to know he was hers...for at least the next few hours.

The elevator took them down several levels to the lowest passenger deck, the Riviera, which surprised Paige. She'd just assumed Harrison would be in one of the luxurious veranda suites, similar to hers. She was even more surprised when he opened the door to his cabin and she stepped inside. The shoebox-size room, while adequate for one person, was bare to the bone in the comfort department.

"Why are you staying in such a small cabin?" she asked with absolutely no tact before she could stop herself.

Her question created a flash of unease in Harrison, which he quickly masked. "It was sort of a last-minute deal," he answered offhandedly. "This was the only thing available. Of course, I wasn't planning on entertaining."

"But if the cruise line really wanted your money, they'd surely do better than this," she persisted. "They should wine and dine you, treat you like a prince. You don't even have a porthole!"

"I wanted to experience what the average passenger does. I didn't want to be treated like a VIP." Harrison was clearly impatient with her focus on his accommodations. He slid his hand beneath her hair to the back of her neck and pulled her close. "I have a double bed...and you. What man needs more luxury than that?"

Nice sentiment, she thought skeptically. But there was something wrong here. Harrison hadn't told her the whole truth about himself. No matter what his excuses, this wasn't the sort of room a wealthy financier would put up with.

She started to argue further, but he kissed her again, a long, languid kiss that turned her insides to warm molasses. What did it matter if he kept secrets from her? If they'd been contemplating a serious relationship, that would be one thing. But a shipboard fling? They owed each other nothing.

An insistent voice inside her argued that it was wrong to trivialize her relationship with Harrison as a "fling," but Paige didn't listen. Harrison was exploring her mouth with his tongue and tracing her sensitive ear with one curious fingertip, and lucid thought was rapidly becoming an impossibility.

Last night, everything had happened so suddenly there was no time for savoring the bombardment of sensations. This time Harrison clearly had a more leisurely plan in mind. Paige closed her eyes and soaked up his attentions like a sponge, acutely aware of his every caress, every breath that warmed her cheek, every murmured word of endearment.

Her stretchy knit top had a row of buttons down the back. Harrison began unfastening them one by one, baring her shoulders to the cool, air-conditioned air. She stood still as a statue, letting him undress her inch by delicious inch. Then he kissed every place he bared, sometimes merely brushing his lips against her skin, other times teasing her with his tongue and teeth.

He opened the front clasp of her bra, and her breasts, aching for his touch, spilled into his eager hands. He lavished them with attention until Paige wanted to weep with the glory of it.

A spark ignited somewhere deep inside her, quickly growing into a sphere of heat, continuing to expand until it stole up her chest and neck, down her arms and legs. He circled her navel with her tongue, while he pulled her shorts and panties down her hips in one liquid silk motion.

She was already light-headed and feverish. She was going to faint if his kisses moved any lower.

Perhaps sensing that her knees were going to give way any moment, he swept her into his arms and deposited her gently on the bed. She expected him to join her there, or at least to sit on the edge of the mattress and take off his own clothes. But he surprised her by stepping away from her, then staring at her with eyes that could almost burn her with their intensity.

His concentrated scrutiny, which appeared to take in every freckle on her body, made her suddenly nervous, and she fretted a bit with the sheet, fighting the urge to cover herself.

"I don't mean to embarrass you," he said, immediately picking up on her mood. He worked at his own shirt buttons as he spoke, then yanked it off. "It's just that I don't think I could ever get my fill of looking at you." He kicked off his deck shoes. His khaki trousers went next, dispensed with in a series of quick, jerky motions.

Finally, still standing far out of her reach, he took off his briefs, revealing the full extent of his desire for her. The sight of him, trim and muscular and pulsating with vitality, literally took her breath away.

They stared at each other for uncounted seconds, and Paige got the distinct impression that Harrison was…memorizing her? Then it hit her. This was to be their last time together. For whatever private reasons Harrison had, he did not want to continue their relationship beyond today.

Perhaps he was starting to feel those first tender stirrings of love, too, and he didn't want to dig himself any deeper. Or maybe he sensed the depths of Paige's feelings—which wouldn't be all that hard, as transparent as she was sometimes—and he was trying to save her from her own runaway heart by breaking things off early and cleanly. Whatever his reasons, Paige knew without a doubt that was Harrison's plan. It was amazing how well she'd come to know him in the short time since they'd met. She could read so much, now, in those expressive brown eyes.

Just when she thought she couldn't take the distance between them a moment longer he came to her.

What had started as a visual feast became a banquet of tactile sensations as he began a thorough exploration of her body with his hands and his mouth. Paige discovered excruciating sensitivity in places she'd never imagined...behind her knees, at the base of her throat. Even her eyelids were awash with sensation when Harrison kissed them.

The feel of his body pleasured her in surprising ways, too. She reveled in the differing textures—the coarse hair on his chest, the slight scratch of his beard, the hard muscles beneath velvet skin on his back.

His caresses became more bold. Butterfly-light kisses on the inside of her thighs—and the more intimate kisses, too—drove her almost beyond reason, until she was literally begging him to put an end to her sweet misery.

He didn't. Instead he covered her body with his and entered her, slowly at first, testing, then suddenly filling her with a powerful thrust, enhancing her pleasure with the purely emotional joy of the union of their bodies.

Grasping her hips, he pulled them flush against his, driving more deeply than she'd ever felt a man inside her before. Then he began a slow, hypnotic rhythm of in and out.

She could feel him everywhere—his chest hair abrading her sensitive nipples, his breath hot against her neck, his hands caressing even as he continued to guide their movements. Time stood still as they traveled to some distant plane, where they existed solely to please each other.

With one final thrust he cried out something—it might have been her name—and slumped against her. Although she was a sigh away from following him, she deliberately held back, wanting to savor his climax, when all barriers dropped away and she could see the pure, unguarded Harrison. She wanted to absorb every nuance about him during this moment of heightened pleasure between them.

She would have liked for them to stay joined longer, but he quickly withdrew and buried his face in her hair. "Paige, I'm sorry."

"Sorry?" she asked, bewildered.

"I couldn't . . . I didn't wait for you."

"Oh, that." She ran her fingers through his hair. "That was my fault, really. I held back because I wanted to enjoy your pleasure." Seeing that he didn't understand, she tried again. "The fireworks don't matter to me. The important thing is the closeness, the sharing. I don't have to . . . what are you doing?"

He'd started by rubbing her abdomen, but his fingers had wandered lower, tangling in the curls at the apex of her thighs, then slipping between her legs, where she was slick and wet and a bit tender from their recent lovemaking. "Fireworks," he said, raising his head and flashing a wicked grin.

"But I...but we're..."

"Done? I don't think so."

"But you don't have to—"

"Honey, this is not an obligation. There is nothing that would make me happier than to watch you...peak. Not even my own satisfaction—fantastic as that was—can compare." He slid one finger inside her and she gasped with pleasure.

"What if I don't?" she objected weakly.

"You will. Even if it takes hours."

Typical male ego, she thought, determined to see his woman satisfied. It didn't take hours, of course. In fact, although she didn't actually look at her watch, she thought it took about half a minute. So he slowly, determinedly, brought her to another peak of pleasure. And then they made love again, exhausting themselves in the most enjoyable fashion Paige could imagine.

Several hours later, after they'd missed even the late dinner seating, Paige realized she had never felt so close to another human being as she did to Harrison. No matter how she'd tried not to, she had fallen in love. She would never be the same.

They got under the covers and dozed fitfully. Later they woke, unable to sleep, and Harrison became talkative—and uncharacteristically philosophical.

"Have you ever done something you regret?" he asked out of the blue.

"Sure, I think everybody does," she answered in a sleepy voice. "Sometimes I regret that I didn't study hard enough in college so I could get into medical school. Still, I like what I'm doing now."

"Medical school? You wanted to be a doctor?"

"Oh, briefly. But I guess I didn't want it that badly."

"What about more recently?" he persisted. "Have you ever gotten involved in something you didn't mean to, then gotten in over your head?"

"You mean about us," she concluded. "Harrison, I don't regret—"

"Not us. I'm talking about something else, something, oh, perhaps a bit unethical? Something you couldn't get out of once you'd started?"

Paige couldn't imagine what he was getting at, unless he was about to make some sort of confession. She obliged him by trying to answer his question, hoping that if she opened up, he might do the same. "Well, I guess I regret butting into my mother's life. I should never have agreed to travel with her under false pretenses. Although I'm not sorry I came on the cruise. It's turned out...much more interesting than I'd anticipated."

Harrison didn't respond to her deliberately provocative tone. "You know," he said, following his own conversational agenda, "it's never too late to turn back, to tell the truth and undo the damage. It might not be as hard as you think. And there are people to help you, people who care about you."

Paige was utterly bewildered. What in the world was he getting at? "I already told my mother the truth— accidentally. But then I was glad it was out in the open. She took it pretty well." Paige paused, then continued. "Is there something you regret, Harrison? Anything you'd like to undo?"

A long silence stretched between them. "No," he finally answered, his voice bleak.

The man was utterly infuriating. He was holding something back, no doubt about it. But whatever reassurance he'd been seeking from her, she apparently hadn't provided it, because he wasn't about to confide in her.

She knew she shouldn't let it bother her, but it did. After what they'd just shared, she would have told him anything, trusted him with anything, even her life. But the feeling wasn't mutual.

Damnation! She'd fallen in love with a man who was living a lie. The wrong man. Perhaps even a con man. She'd gone and followed in her mother's footsteps.

Paige was almost relieved to know Harrison would be the one to end it between them. At least this way the decision wouldn't be hers to make. There was no possibility she would behave like a love-struck fool, dragging some inappropriate man to the altar only to pay the price in heartache later.

Instead she was paying the price right now, and it was dear.

"What time is it?" she asked.

Harrison picked up his watch from the nightstand and showed it to her. The illuminated dial told her it was after midnight.

"I should go."

"So soon?"

"Aurora will be worried," she said, although nothing could be farther from the truth. Aurora would be congratulating herself for helping her daughter find a man, and smiling secretly, knowing exactly why Paige hadn't shown up for dinner.

But Paige had to leave. She would never be able to spend the night with Harrison, knowing their parting was looming closer and closer. She had to get it over with.

"If you feel you have to," Harrison said, sounding as depressed as she felt. Still, though, he was every inch the gentleman. He got up and gathered her clothes from the floor. He fastened the buttons on the back of her shirt, but there were no kisses, no playfulness. He was ready for her to leave, she realized, fighting back utter desolation.

He started to put on his own clothes.

"Don't," she said. "There's no need for you to walk me back to my cabin."

"Of course there's a need. You expect me to just turn you out into the night?"

"I'd prefer it that way. I need some time to... decompress."

"All right," he agreed, almost too easily.

Harrison never turned the light on, and she was glad. She didn't want to see his face, and she most certainly didn't want him to see hers. He kissed her softly and bade her good-night. "Sleep well."

He made no mention of seeing her the next day, or at any time, for that matter.

Harrison lay awake long after Paige was gone. He'd done it again. He'd fallen in love with a criminal. Was there some tragic flaw in his makeup that drew him to such women?

He'd been willing to go to bat for Paige. If only she had confided in him, he would have helped her and Aurora through the nightmare they were about to encounter. Who knows, he might even have helped them escape prosecution—he was that crazy about Paige. But though he'd given her every opportunity, she hadn't confessed.

He had no choice but to continue with his plan to pursue justice, no matter how harsh. He supposed he ought to have been grateful that Paige hadn't tested his ethics. For the love of a woman, he might have failed miserably.

The next morning Aurora, anxious for a day of shopping on Grand Cayman, had to prod Paige out of bed. "What happened to that chipper little robin who was always out of bed at the crack of dawn?" Aurora chided her daughter. "Could it be she was out carousing a bit late last night?"

"Knock it off," Paige grumbled as she crawled out of bed.

Aurora snapped her mouth shut, cutting short her teasing. "Paige, honey, is something wrong?"

"Nothing some shopping and sight-seeing won't cure." And maybe a gallon of frozen margaritas.

"Well, I'll agree with you there. Shopping can cure almost anything...especially when I've got your father's credit card."

"You have Daddy's—" Paige stopped herself. Although she thought it was pretty callous for her mother to sponge off Bobby when she was wooing Doc Waller as a prospective husband, Paige decided to keep her opinion to herself. Bobby was the one who allowed it, after all, so it was none of her business.

"After this latest stunt of Bobby's, I think he deserves to finance a healthy shopping spree," Aurora said. "Don't you?"

Paige didn't respond. Instead, she yawned and said, "Give me fifteen minutes and I'll be ready."

Paige's lightning-fast shower made her feel only marginally better. She emerged from the bathroom in her robe, wondering fuzzily what she should wear. Shoot, what did it matter? She reached to open the closet, stopping when she saw Aurora standing in front of the dresser mirror wearing the rhinestone necklace.

"Oh, I've been meaning to give that back to you," Paige said. "I found it in the beach bag, and then I forgot all about it. Where'd you get it, anyway? I've never seen you wear it. It's pretty."

Aurora turned, looking perplexed. "You've never seen me wear it because it's not mine," she objected. "I thought it was yours, although I have to admit it's not your usual style."

"Mother, it has to be yours," Paige reasoned. "You probably left it in the beach bag ages ago and forgot all about it."

"I'm telling you, I've never seen this thing before in my life. I would have remembered it." She took off the glittering necklace and walked over to the sliding glass door, where she could get a better look at it in the light. She turned it this way and that, then gasped. "Paige, I think these stones are the real thing!"

"Oh, Mother, that's ridiculous. If those were real, the necklace would be worth a small fortune."

"But look! The settings are eighteen-karat white gold, it says so right here. No one mounts fake stones in real gold."

Paige walked over and examined the necklace. Sure enough, it was marked as real gold. Her heart skipped a beat. "How would something like this get in your beach bag?"

"I don't know! Someone must have put it there by mistake. Maybe my bag got mixed up with someone else's...well, however it happened, the owner must be frantic. We'd better turn it in right away."

"Yes, you're right. Just let me get dressed."

As Paige randomly yanked a shorts outfit from the closet, someone knocked sharply on the door.

"Oh, that's probably breakfast," Aurora said, laying the necklace on the dresser and heading for the door. She opened it, revealing two stern-looking uniformed men who did not appear to be waiters. Paige peeked around the corner at them, clutching her robe more tightly about her.

One of the men consulted a piece of paper. "Aurora Cheevers? And Paige Stovall?"

"Yes," both women said together.

"What can we do for you?" Paige asked coolly, coming forward. She didn't like the looks of these men. They weren't wearing the customary smiles found on virtually every other crew member she'd encountered.

"The captain has ordered our security director to take you both to the captain for questioning."

Questioning? Panic rose into Paige's throat. It was then that she saw James lurking in the background. "James?" she said in a voice that didn't sound quite like hers. "What's this all about?"

"I'm sorry, ladies," James said sheepishly, "but you'll have to come with me. Captain's orders. And these men will search your cabins."

"Search our—" Paige was so nonplussed she didn't know what to say. "Why?" was all she managed.

"I'll discuss it with you shortly," he said.

One of the men reached for Paige, as if to bodily drag her out of the cabin.

She jerked back. "Wait a minute! Can I at least get dressed? Or do you intend to parade me through the ship in my bathrobe?"

"No, you can't get dressed," James said, refusing to meet her gaze. "Not unless I come in and keep an eye on things while you do. We can't take the chance of your disposing of evidence."

"What evidence?" she demanded, becoming more incensed by the moment.

"Paige, I think we'd better just do as they say," Aurora said calmly. "There's obviously been some sort of mistake made. The sooner we cooperate, the sooner we can get this cleared up."

Paige saw the wisdom in that. She took several deep breaths to calm herself. "Fine. Let's go, then." She managed to step into her slippers before leaving the cabin.

James escorted them to the elevators. People stopped and stared at Paige in her bathrobe, whispering to each other. It was like one of those nightmares Paige had from time to time, in which she showed up at school or church in her underwear, except this time she knew she was very much awake.

James used a special key to take them down to the lowest deck, where passengers weren't normally allowed. On the elevator Paige began to tremble. This was worse than a nightmare. They were on a ship in foreign waters, and they were obviously suspected of some wrongdoing. She had no idea what their legal rights were.

"So, you're the ship's security director," Paige said to James, hoping to provoke some information out of him. "Funny you didn't mention that little detail earlier."

James said nothing.

"Does this have something to do with the necklace, do you think?" Aurora asked Paige in a loud stage whisper as they all stepped off the elevator.

James came to a screeching halt, suddenly interested. "What necklace is that, Aurora?"

"Mother, don't say another word until we find out what this is all about," Paige warned, leery of saying anything that would unwittingly incriminate them. And she had to agree, this probably was connected to the necklace. If someone was trying to railroad them, Paige was determined not to help them do it. She turned to James. "If we're going to be charged with something, I want the services of an attorney."

"An attorney?" Aurora repeated. "For, heaven's sake, Paige, we haven't done anything wrong. Why do we need a lawyer? If we just answer their questions truthfully, I'm sure this will all be cleared up in minutes."

That was Aurora, eternally optimistic, believing the best of everyone.

James didn't respond to Paige's request for legal assistance. Silent and stoic, he led them through a secured door and into a small room, where Captain Barnes was waiting for them. Previously Paige had thought him a cute, grandfatherly man with a ready smile. But the way he was scowling at them now, he wasn't cute at all. In fact, he was downright scary.

James sat down next to the captain.

"Ladies, have a seat," the captain said. "I'm sure you both know what this is all about."

"On the contrary, we have no idea what this is about," Paige said disdainfully. Aurora obediently sat down, but Paige remained standing.

The captain rose slowly, menacingly, out of his chair. "Young lady, you're about to be charged with a very serious crime. I don't take kindly to thieves on my ship. And might I remind you that on the *Caribbean Mermaid*, I am police, prosecutor, judge and jury all rolled into one. I can confine you to your cabins or throw you in the brig. I can put you off the ship, or I can hold you in custody and have you transported back to Liberia, our country of registry, for arrest and prosecution. So I would advise you to cooperate—and to treat me with appropriate respect. Do I make myself clear?"

Paige's knees gave out and she more or less fell into her chair. "Yes, sir."

The captain reclaimed his seat, too. "All right, then. Mermaid Cruise Line has hired a private investigator to look into a series of jewel thefts which have occurred on several different cruises, on all of which you, Mrs. Cheevers, have been a passenger. I, however, was not prepared to make these serious charges on mere suspicion. I wanted proof."

He paused dramatically, then continued. "The investigator has provided compelling evidence against both of you. And if the search of your cabins turns up any of the stolen jewelry..."

Paige shut out the rest as her mind worked furiously. Her mother, a jewel thief? That was the most preposterous thing she'd ever heard. But how did that necklace get in Aurora's beach bag? Obviously someone had planted it there, intending to frame Aurora.

Someone knocked at the door and James answered it. Harrison Powell entered the already-crowded room, looking like he wanted to spit nails, and Paige felt a tidal wave of relief. Harrison would not allow this injustice to continue. He was her white knight, ready to save the damsels in . . .

He shook the captain's hand, then turned to face Paige and her mother, his eyes filled with a mixture of contempt and pity.

Paige's heart dropped into her feet. Oh, no, not . . . How could she have been so stupid, so naive? Harrison was no white knight; he was in cahoots with these blackguards. Then she put it together. He had to be the private eye the captain had referred to.

It was all a lie, then. Harrison had never been genuinely interested in her as a woman. His ardent pursuit of her, his tender kisses, the incredible sex . . . all of it had been nothing but a good acting job, part of some cockeyed investigation.

Tears pressed behind her eyes, but she held them back. She would not humiliate herself further. Instead she stared back at him defiantly. Let him think their brief affair meant as little to her as it obviously did to him.

Nine

Harrison felt sick. Lying to Paige had been bad enough; facing up to what he'd done was excruciating. He tried to read her expression and discern just how badly he'd hurt her. But as she gazed on him disdainfully with eyes as cold as emerald chips, he saw no evidence of pain. All he could see was her condemnation.

Why was he even worried about her feelings? he wondered. She'd brought this on herself. She was involved in a dishonorable undertaking, and she had no right to expect honorable treatment.

Ah, hell, he was just trying to rationalize his own less-than-sterling behavior.

"So we'll be questioning each of you separately," the captain was saying. He turned to James. "Mr. Blair, if you'll escort Miss Stovall to one of the holding cells, we'll begin with Mrs. Cheevers."

Paige stood, her back as stiff and straight as a two-by-four, her head held high. Somehow she managed a positively regal bearing, even in her prim cotton bathrobe—the same bathrobe she'd been wearing the first night they'd made love.

Harrison tore his gaze away from Paige and focused his attention on her mother. For the first time since he'd met her, Aurora looked every one of her fifty-eight years. Her complexion was pale and translucent, her eyes wide and frightened. Her expression was one of total bewilderment. At that moment, it was hard to believe she was a savvy jewel thief.

Captain Barnes, who happened to be a former Marine MP, had asked Harrison to be present for this interrogation solely as a witness. Still, even though he didn't have to ask the questions, Harrison's heart went out to Aurora. Any man with an ounce of compassion would have felt the same way, he was sure.

Aurora, her voice shaking, answered the question as Harrison might have expected. She said she'd found a necklace in Paige's cabin that morning, and that neither of them had any idea how it had gotten into their possession.

"Who could forget a ring like that?" Aurora replied when asked about Mrs. Janks's missing emerald. "But I only saw it the one time—three nights ago, I believe it was. I assure you I haven't seen it since—" A knock on the door interrupted her.

"Come in," Barnes called curtly.

The door opened, and the men who'd been searching Aurora's and Paige's suite came in. One of them handed the captain two clear plastic evidence bags. One held the sapphire-and-diamond necklace, the other an emerald ring.

"The necklace was lying on the dresser in Miss Stovall's cabin, in plain sight," the man said. "The ring was in Mrs. Cheevers's cabin, underneath the mattress."

Aurora's eyebrows flew up in apparent surprise, while the captain stretched his mouth into a grim line.

"Did you find a gold money clip?" Harrison asked.

The men both shook their heads.

"What about lock picks or a glass cutter? Or gloves?"

"No, nothing like that."

"Thank you, that'll be all," the captain said brusquely. He turned back to Aurora. "Would you care to explain how this jewelry came to be in your suite, Mrs. Cheevers?"

She shook her head helplessly. "I have no idea." Her story remained consistent no matter how many times she told it, giving Harrison the first real doubts he'd had regarding Aurora's guilt. Was it even remotely possible someone had framed her?

"Mrs. Cheevers," the captain said, "I'm not interested in seeing you or your pretty daughter incarcerated in a Liberian jail. All I want is to recover the stolen property or adequate compensation, and we'll forget about criminal charges. Make it easy on yourself."

Aurora had blanched at the mention of Liberian jails, but she didn't back down. "I've told you all I know."

Barnes shook his head in disgust. "Fine, then. That's all for now. I'll have one of the men take you back to—"

"Uh, Captain," Aurora interrupted, "might I have a private word with Mr. Powell?"

The two men exchanged glances, and Harrison nodded.

"Fine," the captain said. "I'll see what's keeping Mr. Blair."

The moment they were alone, Aurora rose from her chair and walked over to Harrison until they were standing only inches apart. She stared at him, contemplating. Then all at once, before he had a chance to anticipate it, she slapped him.

He was too surprised to do anything but stare at her with watering eyes, his face stinging.

"That's for Paige," Aurora said, "because she's too much of a lady to do it herself."

She turned her back on him and reclaimed her chair, then calmly studied her manicure.

Harrison knew there was no point in trying to explain anything. He turned and strode from the room.

The captain, waiting outside, looked at Harrison curiously but didn't ask what Aurora had said to him. "James was called away to handle an emergency in the kitchen. What do you say we get some lunch and resume the interrogation afterward?"

Harrison nodded. He was dying to take a break from this ordeal. "I think I'll skip lunch, though," he said. This whole morning had caused him to lose his appetite.

Paige's holding cell consisted of a bench, a concrete floor and four bare walls that seemed to be closing in on her. It was so small she couldn't even pace.

The man who was stationed outside her door had informed her that Aurora's interrogation was over, but Paige wasn't allowed to see her. She hoped her mother was holding up. Aurora was more fragile than she looked, especially when someone deliberately attacked her.

Paige had asked to make a phone call and been denied. No one had offered her any food, either, and she hadn't eaten for almost twenty-four hours. That was probably a good thing, she realized. The ship was docked, bobbing up and down on one rhythmic swell after another, and she was starting to feel ill.

Someone tapped on the door, then cracked it open. "Paige?"

She froze. The voice was Harrison's. Oh, God, she didn't want to see him or talk to him. She kept her back turned and crossed her arms. "Go away."

She heard him step into the cell. "I brought you some things—some clothes and shoes, your hairbrush. And a sandwich. I thought you might be hungry."

"You thought wrong. Leave me alone."

He touched her shoulder.

She pulled away as if she'd been burned, then whirled around to confront him. "What's your angle this time? Am I supposed to be grateful for your small kindness? Are you perhaps expecting a spontaneous confession? Well, forget it. They can toss me in a dungeon and throw away the key, and I still wouldn't accept anything from you." She pointedly ignored the shopping bag he held out to her.

He set it down. "I had a job to do. That's why I lied to you about who I was."

"You don't have to spell it out to me. I know perfectly well why you did what you did. You're on the side of law and order, and anything's permissible when you're trying to catch a thief, right?" Paige's voice dripped with sarcasm. "Well, all I know is I'll be able to sleep at night. I'm not sure you will."

She saw by the pained expression on his face that her barb had hit its mark, and for a moment she felt guilty. But only a moment. She had to remind herself that he was a superb actor. He'd convinced her he was falling in love with her, hadn't he? Whatever response he was trying to get from her now, she was determined not to give it.

"Will you go, please?"

"I wish you would just listen to me for a minute," he said patiently.

"Why, so you can tell me more lies? I should never have listened to you in the first place, you and your pretty words about how special I am, how beautiful. Like a good-looking millionaire playboy is really going to fall for a short, redheaded dietitian with an attitude. You must have thought I was the dumbest, most gullible woman on the face of the earth."

"I thought nothing of the sort. I care about you, Paige. I care what happens to you. I'm not that good an actor."

She didn't soften one iota. "If you cared anything about me, you'd find out who really stole that necklace, instead of helping James and the captain railroad my mother and me."

"Paige . . ." He seemed to drag the next words out of himself. "Don't you think it's remotely possible that your mother is guilty? She's the only passenger who was on every cruise where jewelry was stolen. I've investigated her background, and she lives well above her means."

Paige closed her eyes, grappling for composure. "No," she said through gritted teeth, "it is not even remotely possible. She lives beyond her means because my father gives her money—lots of it. But aside from that, Aurora is absolutely incapable of dishonesty.''

''Is that why she lies about her age? And about the fact that she's your mother, and not your aunt? Is that why—''

''All right,'' Paige interrupted. ''All right. So maybe she does tell little white lies, in the name of vanity. But she would never do anything illegal. She would never steal, for heaven's sake.''

''Paige, she was charged with shoplifting several years ago.''

''She . . . what?'' This was news to Paige. Feeling queasy again, she stumbled to the bench and sank onto it.

''It was six or seven years ago, probably when you were in college. The charges were dropped.''

''Then we don't know that she did it.'' But Paige's argument sounded weak, even to her. It couldn't be true. Her mother couldn't be a thief! Then a terrible thought occurred to her. She turned to Harrison, full of accusation. ''You're making this up. Divide and conquer, that's what you're trying to do. You're trying to fill me with doubts about my mother. Well, it's not going to work. If you think I'm going to turn against Aurora and present you with some incriminating evidence, you're crazy.''

Harrison joined her on the bench, resting his elbows on his knees. He looked tired. ''I hate to tell you this, Paige, but we don't need any further evidence. Unless something changes in the next few hours, you're both going to Liberia for prosecution. I only

came here because I wanted to explain my side of it.''
He sighed. ''And I did a lousy job of that, I guess.''

''I'll say.'' She wished he weren't sitting so close. At
this distance, it was all too easy for her to remember
why she'd fallen for him in the first place—why she'd
been such an easy target. As furious as she was with
him, he still drew her.

''Will you go, please?'' she said in a small voice,
before she could weaken any further.

''Okay,'' Harrison said, sounding defeated. ''Is
there anything else I can get you? Anything I can do
for you?''

A sharp retort was on the tip of her tongue. But her
pride warred with her fear. She was in real trouble
here, and Harrison was in a position to help her. ''Will
you call my father?'' she asked, half-afraid he would
say no. ''Tell him what's happened.'' If anyone could
get them out of this mess, Bobby could.

''Of course I will. What's the number?''

She rattled off the number of his answering service
from memory. ''Tell them it's an emergency. They'll
know where to find him.''

Harrison had nothing on which to write the number, so he repeated it a couple of times, then retreated
with one last, sad smile, full of regret.

The rest of the day went by in a painful blur for
Harrison. He couldn't get hold of Bobby Stovall, who
was apparently in transit from Hollywood to New
York. The best he could do was leave a complicated
message that he knew would get garbled.

Later, Harrison had to force himself to sit in on
Paige's interrogation, knowing his presence was ag-
gravating the situation and causing her to be less co-

operative. The less cooperative she was, the more irate Captain Barnes got.

She might have escaped prosecution. The evidence pointed mainly at Aurora, and Harrison had his doubts now that Paige was involved. When she said she'd believed the necklace to be costume, her words had the ring of truth about them. But she blew any chance for leniency when she called the captain a weasel.

At the last minute Harrison had pleaded with Barnes to go easy on the two women. Hadn't they suffered enough? Some of the jewelry had been recovered, and it wasn't likely the rest would be, so what was the point of pressing charges? But the captain, not an easy man, hadn't backed down.

Things went downhill from there. The ladies were paraded through the ship—in handcuffs, no less—to board a launch that would take them to Georgetown, Grand Cayman. They would remain on the island, in confinement, until transport to Liberia could be arranged.

Harrison watched from a distance, sick at heart. The ship's security officers assisted Paige and Aurora aboard the small boat. Other onlookers surrounded him, speculating as to why the two women had been arrested.

Even from this distance, Harrison could see that all the fight had gone out of Paige. He could tell by her defeated posture and by the sad, bewildered look on her face. And all the while a question kept nagging at Harrison.

If Aurora had stolen the necklace, why hadn't she hidden it better? Why had she blithely loaned her beach bag to Paige, knowing the necklace was secreted in the side pocket? Of course, it was possible the whole rigmarole about the beach bag was a smoke screen Paige had invented to shift guilt away from herself. But if she was party to the theft, then why would she leave the necklace sitting around in plain sight for anyone to find?

Why hadn't the necklace been hidden under a mattress, like the ring?

Harrison wondered if Paige had taken her seasickness pills. Probably not. He doubted she'd put on any sun block, either. By the time she arrived on the island, she would be sunburned and nauseous, in addition to being scared to death.

It was at that moment that Harrison decided he needed to do something. If there was even a remote chance that one or both of the ladies were innocent, he had to help them bring out the truth. Hell, he was sick to death of this blasted ship, anyway. He would go to Georgetown and see if he could scare up some kind of legal help. Maybe a bond could be posted, although he had no idea who could authorize such a thing. But he could at least try.

He turned away from the railing, intent on packing up his things and finding a way off the ship, when he ran smack into James.

"Where the hell have you been?" Harrison demanded uncharitably.

"Good God, it was awful," James said, oblivious to Harrison's black mood despite his irritated scowl. "One of the cooks decided to go berserk, and the man doesn't speak a word of English, which made negotiating with him a tad difficult. Before we were done there was a full-fledged riot going on in the kitchen. One chef had a pot of hollandaise poured over his head, another was assaulted with a leg of lamb, and I narrowly missed being hit with a flying saucepan.

"I would have thrown them all in the brig, except then I don't know what we would have served the passengers in the way of food. Eventually I managed to get everybody calmed down, apologies made and accepted. Couldn't get away till about five minutes ago. I still don't know what the fight was about."

As he'd offered this lengthy and unwelcome explanation, he'd been watching the boat carrying Paige and Aurora rev its engines and cast off. "So, the lady cat burglars are being dragged away in chains, eh?"

"You don't have to sound so damn cheerful about it," Harrison said.

"Why not? That's one huge problem off my list. In fact, you need to be paid. I'll put in a check requisition today, plus the bonus we promised if the thief was caught."

Two lives were being ruined, and all James cared about were his petty problems. "Don't you feel sorry for them at all?" Harrison asked.

James thought for a moment, then shook his head. "Nah. They're criminals. They're getting what they deserve. You're too soft, Harrison. I've said that from the beginning."

"How can I get off the ship and to Grand Cayman?" Harrison asked abruptly.

"What, you're tired of our hospitality?" James asked with an irritating smile. "You can stay on for the rest of the cruise, you know."

"I just want to know how to get to Grand Cayman."

"Well, a tender boat should be returning later this afternoon. You can hitch a ride back to shore. But, hey, you got a couple of hours. Why don't we go someplace and have a beer? You know, celebrate a successful operation?''

Harrison started to beg off, then shrugged. "Sure, why not?" Now that his assignment was officially over, he could get drunk if he wanted to. And maybe he should. He could get rip-roaring plowed and forget about those scared, jewel green eyes.

The two men sat in one of the lounges, nearly deserted at this hour, and drank, although Harrison only sipped disinterestedly at his beer, while James downed two mugs in quick succession. Every once in a while someone called him on the radio that was strapped to his belt, and he would answer a question or quickly defuse a potentially troublesome situation with a few words of wisdom. James Blair might be an annoying little jerk, Harrison concluded, but he seemed to be pretty good at his job.

"Are you allowed to drink on duty?" Harrison asked.

James shot him an amused look. "You are so straight, Powell. I can't believe what a goody two-shoes you are. No, technically I'm not supposed to drink on duty, and the captain would probably string me up by my toes if he knew. But, hell, after a day like today, I need a brew. It's not like a couple of beers are going to interfere with my ability to do my job.''

Harrison shrugged. In his experience, people who broke small rules were pretty quick to break big ones, too. But it was really none of his business if James wanted to drink on duty.

"You know," James said, chuckling, "you're so straight, it's amazing to me that you ever managed to get into Paige's cabin—or that you knew what to do once you got there.''

Harrison set down his half-empty mug with a bang. He wasn't going to discuss this with James or anybody. What had gone on in Paige's cabin, and in his, was no one else's business. He started to excuse himself, but James, enamored of his own voice at this point, continued.

''When were you able to search the cabin? After she fell asleep?''

''I didn't have to search very hard.''

''Oh, and you just happened to know right where to look.'' James's eyes took on a speculative gleam. ''I suppose Paige talked in her sleep and told you the necklace was in the beach bag?''

Harrison went still inside. How the hell did James know about the beach bag? Harrison had found the necklace lying on the dresser, in plain sight. He hadn't known anything about a beach bag until Paige was questioned. And James hadn't been present.

''The beach bag was just a lucky guess,'' Harrison said, playing along as his mind worked furiously. ''What did the captain have to say about your kitchen riot? I expect he wanted to throw a few people in the brig himself.''

''I haven't talked to him, and I'm not going to. The less said about that, the better.''

So, James hadn't talked to the captain, which was the only other way he could have known about the beach bag. Harrison wanted to kick himself. He and James had meticulously gone over crew and passenger records to find the one person who had been aboard every cruise that experienced a burglary. But James's records hadn't been included. It had never occurred to Harrison to suspect the very man who'd hired him.

The conclusion was inescapable: James could only know about the beach bag if he'd put the necklace there himself. He had a passkey. He could have stolen both pieces of jewelry—quite easily—and planted them to implicate Paige and Aurora. Of course, there was the veranda door, cut with a glass cutter, but Harrison supposed James could have managed that, also, to point the finger of guilt at Aurora.

Harrison was almost shaking with indignation. To think of the hell James had put those two women through! The unconscionable cretin! He didn't know James's motives, and he didn't care. All he knew was that he was going to straighten this mess out right now, even if he had to loosen a few teeth to do it.

"Let's take a walk," he said to James.

James checked his watch. "I have to get back to—"

"It can wait," Harrison said in a tone no one would want to argue with. "I have something important to ask you." And he didn't want to do it around witnesses.

James shrugged and drained the last of his third beer. "All right, but make it quick."

Harrison led the way out of the dimly lit bar and into a corridor. Quickly orienting himself, he headed for the nearest exit that would take them outside.

"Where're we going?" James asked.

"On deck. I don't want anyone to overhear this."

"Ah, sounds like real cloak-and-dagger stuff." James followed willingly, never smelling the trap, as Harrison led him onto the shaded deck and over to the railing. They were at the ship's stern, and straight below them was the churning water created by the *Caribbean Mermaid*'s idling engines.

The area was deserted, which made Harrison's job easier. And James's reflexes were dulled by alcohol— better still. Harrison struck with the quickness of a seabird diving for prey. With one hand he reached behind James, grabbed his arm and wrenched it behind his back. With his other hand he seized James's throat and backed the smaller man up against the railing.

James gave a little "woof" of surprise as most of the air was knocked out of his lungs and he was caught, helpless. His free hand flailed ineffectually against Harrison's shoulder.

"How did you know about the beach bag, you son of a bitch?"

"The beach— What the hell are you talking about?" James squeaked. "Have you gone berserk?"

"No, I'm only just now coming to my senses." Harrison tightened his hold on James's throat. "Now answer my question before I put a permanent kink in your neck. How did you know the necklace was hidden in the beach bag?"

"Th-that's what you told me."

Harrison shook his head. "Uh-uh. I found the necklace out in the open. I knew nothing about a beach bag until a couple of hours ago, during Paige's interrogation."

"Then someone else must have mentioned it," James said quickly. "Paige did. Yes, I'm sure that's it now. When we came to her cabin this morning."

Harrison narrowed his eyes. "She just volunteered this information, out of the blue?"

"Yes! She knew why we were there, and she started jabbering about finding the necklace in Aurora's beach bag, trying to make herself look good."

"I can check out your story, James. But I don't think I will. I think I'll just toss you overboard right now and let the sharks eat you."

James paled beneath his artfully acquired tan. "Have you lost your mind?"

"No, but you're going to lose a few things . . . to the sharks. . .unless I hear the truth out of you pretty fast. You stole that jewelry, didn't you? And as soon as I came up with a suspect, you framed her, right?"

"I don't know what you're—"

"Oh, yes, you do. You used your passkey, and then you tried to make me believe that a sweet lady like Aurora jumped from balcony to balcony and picked locks. But we never found any lock picks or glass cutters, did we? Or any gloves, for that matter." He pushed harder against James's throat until the other man was bent backward over the railing and he was scrabbling for traction with his feet.

"You wouldn't k-kill me," James said, his voice shaking uncontrollably.

He wouldn't, but James didn't have to know that. Hell, James had better believe his life was in danger. If this gamble didn't pay off, Harrison would find himself joining the ladies in that Liberian jail— charged with attempted murder. "If you don't start talking pretty soon, I'll toss you right over this railing. And I'll make everyone believe you jumped. You sent two innocent women to jail, and I'm pretty annoyed."

"Annoyed? You're a flaming maniac, that's what— hey, stop pushing!" James cried, teetering on the railing. "Once and for all, I did not steal any jewelry. Now let me go, for God's sake!"

Harrison had no choice but to release the man. His ploy hadn't worked. Now what was he going to do? Hell, that was a moot question. He wouldn't be able to do anything from the brig.

Ten

The hotel room had carpet and curtains and a private bath, but it was still a prison cell, Paige thought uncharitably. She supposed she should be grateful. At least the room was large enough to accommodate pacing, and she was taking full advantage.

She was beyond scared now. She was furious—at the captain, at the unknown person who had framed them, but mostly at Harrison Powell for cultivating her trust like a delicate orchid, then crushing it under his heel.

"I will never, ever trust a man again as long as I live, and I certainly won't sleep with another one," she said, fuming.

Aurora, lounging on the bed, listlessly reading a tourist magazine, shook her head. "Not all men are like that, honey."

"That's what you said about Curtis Rittenour."

"Curtis who? Oh, that dreadful doctor you were so smitten with. So, okay, there are a lot of rotten ones out there, but there are some good ones, too."

"Name one."

"Your father," Aurora answered without hesitation.

"I thought you were mad at him," Paige said, stopping her pacing for the moment.

Aurora actually smiled. "I'm getting over it. Besides, he's going to get us out of this . . . this situation. Somehow."

"By the time he gets the message you left, we'll be in Liberia. Mother, I'm afraid this is one mess even Bobby Stovall can't bail us out of."

"Well, if he can't, we'll just have to cope. I wonder what the weather is like in Liberia? Do you think we'll need more clothes?"

"We won't need any clothes!" Paige exploded. "We'll be wearing prison stripes and working on a chain gang. They may even execute thieves in Liberia."

"Don't be ridiculous. I look awful in stripes. Besides, I think Liberia's legal system is based on ours in the United States."

Paige looked at her mother in surprise. "How do you know that?"

"Oh, I read it somewhere."

"You seem awfully . . . calm," Paige observed.

Aurora sat up and closed the magazine. "I've lived a lot longer than you have, Paige. Sometimes life throws you a curve. You can moan and groan about it, or you can make the best of it. I am scared, and angry, but I'm trying not to be."

Sometimes her mother surprised her, Paige thought, as she sat down on the bed. Just when she should be falling apart, Aurora was proving to be a veritable rock. "Mother, were you ever charged with shoplifting?"

Aurora's jaw dropped. "For heaven's sake, how did you find out about that?"

"Harrison told me. He dug into your background, trying to find evidence that you were a thief. It's...it's true then?"

"Yes, I was arrested and charged," Aurora huffed, "but the charges were dropped. I accidentally walked out of a store at the mall with a scarf in my hand. You know how I am when I shop."

Paige did know. Her mother was as absentminded as a puppy sometimes—especially at the mall, where she darted from one attraction to another like a kid in a candy store. "How come you never mentioned it?"

"Because I was embarrassed, of course. You would have lectured me. That was another jam your father helped me out of. Oh, for heaven's sake, Paige, you don't really think I stole that jewelry, do you?"

Paige was ashamed to admit, even to herself, that she'd started to harbor a tiny, nagging suspicion. Fortunately a knock on the door prevented her from answering her mother's question.

"Come in," Paige called out, adding under her breath, "as if it matters whether I give permission or not." When the door opened, however, the person who walked through was not the security guard she was expecting. She stared at the tall, silver-haired man in disbelief. "Daddy!"

"Bobby!" Aurora cried out at the same time. She leapt from the bed and launched herself at her ex-husband, nearly knocking him over in her hurry to get her arms around him. "How did you get here so fast? I only left the message a couple of hours ago." Then she burst into tears.

"There, there now, honey, everything's going to be all right. Earlier I got a message from someone else—Hamilton? Harrington?"

"Harrison," Paige said, amazed Harrison had actually done what he'd promised and contacted Bobby. She'd been sure the offer of help was only for show. She walked over and hugged her father, too, inhaling the wonderful, familiar scent of the cologne he always wore. Although his girth had increased over the years and his hair had thinned a bit, Paige still considered him the most handsome man in the world.

"Harrison, that was it," Bobby said, giving his daughter a reassuring squeeze. "The message caught up with me at LaGuardia, so I just hopped the first plane for Grand Cayman. Well, now, how are my two little jailbirds holding up?"

Paige pulled away from the group hug. "Daddy, don't joke. This is serious. They think we're jewel thieves, and they're taking us to Liberia for prosecution. We might spend the rest of our lives in jail!"

"I don't think so, honey. In fact . . ." He extricated himself from Aurora's tenacious grasp and stepped out the open door to peer down the hallway. "Ah, here he comes now."

"Here who comes?" Paige asked, wondering what had happened to the guard stationed outside their door.

"That security fellow. If I'm not mistaken, he's come to give you your walking papers."

Was Bobby saying what she thought he was saying? Paige wondered breathlessly.

She didn't have time to ask. In moments the guard appeared in the doorway wearing a sheepish smile. "Uh, Mrs. Cheevers? Miss Stovall? You're free to go now."

"You mean the captain's changed his mind about Liberia?" Aurora asked, gripping Bobby's arm.

"All charges have been dropped, ma'am. The *Caribbean Mermaid* will be casting off in about an hour. If you hurry, you can make the last tender boat back to the ship."

"Return to the ship?" Paige said in utter horror. "Listen, bud, you'd have to drag me kicking and screaming back to that floating—umph!" Aurora's elbow in her ribs brought her to an abrupt halt.

"Paige, darling, he's telling us we're free. Let's not look a gift horse in the mouth." She turned to the man and gave him one of her more dazzling smiles, though her eyes were still shiny with tears. "Thank you so much, young man. We're looking forward to the rest of the cruise."

When the man had gone and the door was closed, Paige just stood there in stunned silence for a moment. "That's it?" she finally managed. "It's really over?"

"Paige, pay attention!" Aurora said gleefully. She was already starting to pack up her things. "We're free, all charges dropped! Yippee!"

Paige looked at her father with pure admiration. "How did you do it? And so fast?" Bribery was the only thing that came to mind, but she didn't think the captain was the type of man to accept a bribe.

Bobby shrugged. "I wish I could take credit, but I had nothing to do with this. I just happened to over-hear those security guys talking when I was in the lobby."

"Then it had to be Harrison," Paige murmured.

"Harrison? Who is this guy, anyway?" Bobby asked.

"Oh, never mind. I guess it doesn't matter how it happened, as long as they dropped the charges." But she couldn't help remembering what she'd said to Harrison during their last conversation. She'd told him that if he truly cared for her, he would find the real thief. Is that what he'd done?

She returned her attention to Aurora. "You're not seriously thinking of returning to that hell ship, are you?"

"Why not? We still have three days left of the cruise. No sense wasting them."

"Mother! After what they did to us?"

Aurora shrugged. "They made a mistake. What would be the point of dwelling on it or holding a grudge?"

Paige was appalled. "You're entirely too forgiving. I, for one, am going to nurse a grudge the size of Africa, and for a good long time, too. If you're deter-mined to go back to the ship, you'll have to go alone."

"You mean you'd let me rattle around in that huge suite by myself?" Aurora said innocently.

"That's exactly what—" Paige stopped, her mind working furiously. Then she smiled as a wicked thought occurred to her. "Oh, I have a marvelous idea. Daddy, why don't you go with Mother and take my place?"

"Paige, please," Aurora objected, grimacing dramatically. "I don't mind being alone that much."

Bobby chuckled. "Even if your mother would have me, Paige, I've got business to take care of. I'm negotiating a contract to do a Broadway score."

"That can wait, can't it? It's only three days." Paige looked at her mother, pleased to see that Aurora's scowl had been replaced by an almost hopeful expression. This would be too good to be true if Paige could pull it off. Her parents, alone together for three days on a cruise ship?

Finally Bobby smiled at Paige, looking full of mischief. "Did you tell her about our, er, plan?"

"Yes, I'm afraid I did," Paige said. "The truth slipped out accidentally. But she's not really mad."

He looked at his ex-wife. "How about you? Did you let anything 'slip out'?"

"No," Aurora answered hastily, looking quite alarmed. "No, and don't you say a word, not when she's in this kind of mood. She'll kill us."

"Tell me what?" Paige asked, bewildered.

"I'd better hurry if I want to make the tender boat," Aurora said, ignoring Paige. She handed Bobby her suitcase.

"What are you not supposed to tell me?" Paige asked again, this time directing the query to her father.

"I'll see that your mother gets safely back on the ship," Bobby said, also ignoring her question. "Then I need to hustle on back to New York. What about you? What are you planning to do?"

Paige shrugged. It appeared her parents weren't going to let her in on their secret. "Don't worry about me. I'll get some dinner, go to bed early, then in the morning climb on the first plane for home.''

Bobby immediately reached for his wallet. ''You'll need plane fare. And something for the hotel—who knows if this is paid for. And—''

''I can handle it, Daddy.''

''Let me at least buy you dinner. I got you into this whole thing.'' He pressed some bills into her hand, and she stuffed them into the pocket of her shorts without looking at them. ''Thanks, Daddy.''

Paige's parents made a hasty departure, bustling like they were off on a honeymoon. If only they were, she caught herself thinking. They were so perfect for each other.

''Do you want me to tell Harrison anything?'' Aurora asked hopefully as they were going out the door.

''Hah! You must be kidding. If you have to speak to him, tell him I hope he rots in hell.''

''Paige, that's not very nice. Besides, I already slapped him for you. That should be enough.''

Paige gasped. ''You didn't.''

''I'll tell him no hard feelings, okay? He was doing a job, after all, and I imagine he'll feel pretty badly once he finds out we're innocent. And he is a handsome devil, even if he isn't a millionaire. A private investigator wouldn't be such a bad catch.''

''The very idea nauseates me,'' Paige said succinctly. ''I hope he does feel bad. I hope he feels just awful. Now go, you're going to miss the boat.'' She kissed them both on the cheek and sent them on their way.

When she was alone again, Paige wandered aimlessly around the hotel room, looking out the window, picking up the magazine and setting it down, sifting through her suitcase for something to wear to dinner, then abandoning the idea. To go through so much stress and worry and anxiety, only to have their problems end so abruptly, had left her feeling empty and tired.

A change of scenery would help, she decided. So she picked out a hotel at random from the tourist magazine and made a reservation for the night. And since she was on the phone, she made her plane reservations for the following morning.

By the time she'd settled into her new hotel she was starting to get hungry. She considered room service, then decided she really needed to get out. So she forced herself to pick out a sun dress to wear and hung it in the bathroom to steam out the wrinkles while she took a quick shower. Then she dressed, put on makeup and twisted her hair into a French braid. When she ran across the gold filigree necklace Harrison had bought for her in Cozumel, she impulsively put it on.

Nothing she did made her feel any better.

The sun was setting by the time she ordered dinner in a quaint, open-air restaurant that looked out on the harbor. The *Caribbean Mermaid* was casting off. She watched as the ship sailed away, growing smaller and smaller. When it was a mere dot in the distance, she realized why she was feeling so depressed. Harrison was sailing away from her.

Absently she reached up and touched the necklace. She would never see him again.

"Is something wrong with your dinner, ma'am?"

She hadn't even touched the red snapper she'd ordered. "Oh, no, it's fine," she said, taking a dutiful bite. "Thank you."

The waiter nodded and left, but moments later he returned. "Perhaps some wine would make the dinner more palatable?" he said from behind her.

"No, I don't think—" She'd turned around to look at him. Only it wasn't the waiter standing behind her, it was Harrison Powell, holding an open bottle of white wine, two glasses, and a hopeful expression.

Paige's throat squeezed so tight she couldn't speak, couldn't breathe. Harrison! What was he doing here? She was still mad as a whole hive of hornets, but a part of her was actually happy to see him, relieved to know he wasn't on that ship literally sailing away into the sunset.

"I've been looking all over this island for you," he said. "I thought you'd be at the hotel, but they said you'd checked out."

"I checked into another hotel," she said coolly. "I didn't want to be found, not by you or anyone."

"Oh. Mind if I sit down?" he asked with maddening casualness.

"Of course I mind! You're a complete jerk. Get away from me or . . . or I'll scream."

"Don't you even want to hear my side of the story?" he asked, sitting down in the chair opposite her despite her wishes.

"Nothing you could say would excuse your abhorrent, conscienceless behavior." She stared out to sea, willing herself not to cry.

"It might have been abhorrent, but it wasn't conscienceless. Believe me, my conscience almost burned a hole through me." He poured some wine into one of the glasses and set it in front of her, then filled the other for himself. "Don't you even want to know what happened? Why the charges were dropped?"

"I don't care. I'm just glad they were, and I want to forget the whole thing, and you. I especially want to forget you." She immediately regretted the harsh words, when, from the corner of her eye, she saw the effect they had on him. He looked like someone had just kicked him in the gut.

"I wish I could forget you, too, Paige," he said. "But I can't, and I won't. Not for the rest of my life."

She wasn't going to touch that one. "So what did happen?" she asked, her curiosity finally getting the better of her. "Did you find the real thief?"

He nodded. "James. It was James Blair, the man who hired me, the man who was assisting me."

"James?" Paige repeated. "That little slime ball! I knew there was something about him I didn't like." She listened greedily despite herself as Harrison explained how James had allowed Harrison to come up with a suspect, then had worked furiously to make sure that suspect—Aurora—was found guilty.

"Apparently he'd racked up some rather impressive gambling debts in the Bahamas," Harrison explained, "and he was using the jewelry to pay those off. But then the Mermaid higher-ups were putting pressure on him to catch the thief before any bad publicity got out. You and Aurora became his fall guys...er, girls."

"Can I be on the firing squad that executes him?" she asked. Then she thought to ask, "How did you find out it was him?"

"He slipped up, like a lot of criminals do. He wanted to talk about the case, bask in the glow of his success. I spotted an inconsistency in something he said, and from then on it was just a matter of pursuing it."

"So you... questioned him?"

"Well, I threatened to throw him overboard if he didn't tell the truth. And when that didn't work, I dragged him to the captain and explained my suspicions. Thank God, Barnes had enough faith in me, and enough distrust for James, that he agreed to have James's cabin searched. We found Mr. Janks's money clip."

Paige actually laughed for the first time since her nightmare had begun. "I wish I had a picture of the look on James's face when you showed him that." Suddenly she realized she was having a conversation with Harrison, an amiable one, and she was mad at herself for softening toward him.

She had her answers now, and it was time she put an end to this meeting. She pulled out a large bill and laid it on the table by the check the waiter had left. At the same time Harrison threw down a credit card.

"Let me at least buy you dinner," he said.

"No, really, that's okay. I can afford it." When she'd pulled the crumpled bills out of her shorts pocket, she'd discovered that her father had given her five hundred dollars. She could buy one heckuva dinner with that.

Harrison took back his card without arguing. "Let's take a walk, then."

"No. Harrison, there's no point dwelling on any of this. I was naive and gullible, and I got what I deserved. I learned a lesson, and I doubt I'll ever be that trusting again. But I'll survive. So give your conscience a break."

The waiter picked up the check and left her change. She stuffed some of it back in her purse, leaving a generous tip, and stood. "Goodbye, Harrison."

She turned to leave, but he was right behind her.
"Walk with me, Paige," he said softly. "I have a lit-
tle more explaining to do. Then I'll leave you alone.
Please," he added when she didn't answer right away.

If he'd tried to charm her into it, she would have
said no. But she could not resist this earnest appeal,
which made him seem so vulnerable. "All right."

They left the restaurant and walked down a flight of
ancient stone steps, through a dark alleyway and
across a street to the white sand beach. Georgetown
was quite a charming place, with its quaint old build-
ings, lush tropical flowers and breathtaking views in
every direction. Paige hadn't noticed anything about
the island before now. She'd had her mind on other
things.

A few diehard tourists were still frolicking in the
fading light, getting in that last Frisbee throw, but the
beach was mostly deserted at this hour. Paige and
Harrison walked quietly on the hard-packed sand,
close but not touching.

"I haven't done much undercover work in the
past," Harrison began, "and I doubt I'll do any in the
future."

"But why?" Paige couldn't resist asking. "You're
so good at it."

"No, I'm not. The part about being an interna-
tional financier—that was an act. And pretending an
interest in your mother—that was all part of the plan.
Well, of course I found her charming, what man
wouldn't? But I would have taken that flirtation only
so far, and I made that clear to James from the beginning.

"But as for my pursuing you—that was not part of
the plan. And, in fact, I nearly blew the whole thing

because I couldn't keep away from you. You were right, I was chasing two women at the same time, but I only wanted to catch one of them."

Paige said nothing. She didn't understand why he was bothering. She'd absolved him, told him he could be on his way with a clear conscience. Why was he dredging up these painful memories?

"My plan was to get into your cabin. But making love to you wasn't on the agenda. I wouldn't use any woman that way, not for any reason. Especially not you."

"Then why did you do it?" she shot back. "Because I was there," she answered for him. "I was convenient."

"Because you woke up and put the moves on me," he reminded her gently. "I tried to do the gentlemanly thing and give you a graceful out. But you were rather...determined. If you'll recall."

Suddenly she did recall, and her face grew warm.

"But I'm not claiming to be purely a victim of seduction," he continued. "At some point I made the conscious decision to make love to you. And I wasn't sorry, even though I knew the trouble it would cause. It was...well, I guess it would be trite to say this again, that it was wonderful beyond belief. But it was."

Paige didn't think it was trite. No other man had ever said such things to her before. His words made her feel tingly all over.

"I could have searched your cabin and Aurora's ten times over while you slept, but I didn't. I couldn't bring myself to betray your trust like that. I was planning on chucking the assignment first thing in the morning, and then I was going to confess the whole truth to you and take my chances. Then, as I was leaving your cabin, I saw the necklace.

"I couldn't believe it. I couldn't believe you were involved. Your mother, yes. I didn't want to believe that, but I could have. But not you."

"Why not me?" she asked, bewildered.

"Because I'd fallen in love with you," he admitted. "And I just couldn't believe I would fall in love with a thief, not again."

Paige felt as if her every breath had deserted her. Her gullible little heart leapt, wanting to believe him so badly. But her skepticism won out. If he'd fooled her before, he could do so twice. "What do you mean by *again?*" she asked, hoping to buy some time.

He shook his head. "It's a chapter of my life not worth getting into. Let's just say that, because of similar circumstances in the past, I was beginning to doubt my own judgment. Later, I tried to coax you into confessing. Do you remember?"

Now that he mentioned it, she did recall the odd conversation they'd had last night, the baffling questions about regrets, which now made sense. "Yes, I remember," she said. "What would you have done if I'd confessed?"

"I'd have helped you," he answered without hesitation. "I used to be a criminal defense attorney. Hell, it even crossed my mind that I might help you get away with it, if I thought there was a chance you would reform. If I had seen even a small sign of remorse . . . but when you wouldn't confide in me, you left me with no choice but to turn you in."

"I couldn't confide something I knew nothing about," she reasoned.

"Well, of course. I know that now."

Paige stopped and looked up at the sky, counting the stars. What did he want from her? she wondered. Was he trying to avoid a lawsuit? Did he simply want her to believe that he'd meant her no harm, that he hadn't callously taken her to bed and pretended to care for her, all in the interest of bringing her mother to justice?

Maybe that would be the best thing, she reasoned. If she gave him what he wanted, perhaps he would go and leave her in peace. She folded her arms to ward off the sudden chill she felt, then looked at him squarely. "I believe you, Harrison. Now will you please—"

"Oh, thank God."

She wasn't prepared for him to put his arms around her. Too surprised to move, she remained stiff and unyielding, her arms still folded tightly.

"Paige?" he said after a few moments.

"Wh-what?"

"I don't think you really believe me. You're just saying that to get rid of me."

She looked up at him, totally confused. "I don't know what to believe!"

"You can believe this." He leaned down and covered her mouth with his, and Paige unfolded like a flower in the morning sun. In the few short hours since they'd last kissed, she'd almost forgotten how wonderful it was, how it made her feel all warm and bubbly inside. With striking clarity she realized that Harrison couldn't possibly be that good an actor.

She wound her arms around his shoulders and pressed herself against him, reveling in the feel of his hard, unyielding body against hers. She felt not the slightest urge to resist.

He pulled back before the kiss could get out of hand. They were still on a public beach, although no one seemed to be paying the slightest bit of attention to them.

"I don't blame you for being skeptical," he said, brushing her cheek with his. "It's hard to believe I could fall in love with you after knowing you for such a short time. But I am in love with you, Paige. Hopelessly."

"It's not that hard to believe, when I..." Her words trailed off. Hadn't she fallen in love with him just as quickly, just as hopelessly? But she found it difficult to admit that.

He caressed her face and brushed her full lower lip with his thumb. "All I'm asking is that you let me hang around long enough for you to discover who I really am, what I'm really like. And to find out if you could love me back."

"And supposing I could?" she asked, her heart in her throat.

"I'd ask you to marry me."

That clinched it. He couldn't possibly be buttering her up to avoid a lawsuit. What man would choose marriage—a lifetime sentence—over piddling litigation?

"Oh, Harrison, I do love you, and I forgive you, and I'm sorry my mother slapped you," she said, all in a rush.

He looked a little startled that she'd given in so quickly, but then he smiled, making that dark empty beach seem to her as bright as Las Vegas. "In that case, will you marry me?"

"Yes." She laughed with the heady elation of it all. Again, her circumstances had changed so quickly it took her breath away. But this time she was left feeling full to bursting with all good things.

Harrison started to kiss her again, but she held up her finger. "Hold it right there. I have one condition I must insist on."

"What's that?" he asked, grinning. He wasn't the slightest bit fooled by her show of sternness.

"You have to promise that, for our honeymoon, you won't take me anywhere near a cruise ship."

He laughed out loud. "We'll go to the mountains, okay?" Then he did kiss her, and Paige again lost herself in his touch.

Much later, as she lay in Harrison's arms, Paige quietly acknowledged what she'd feared for some time—she was exactly like her mother. She'd met a man on a cruise, and now she was going to marry him.

But somehow, the realization only made her smile. Aurora was right about falling in love. It was an experience Paige wouldn't trade for anything. But unlike Aurora's sometimes fleeting love affairs, this relationship was going to last.

Epilogue

"That must be our pizza," Paige said when she heard the doorbell ring. She and Harrison had spent the better part of the past three days hibernating in her Miami apartment, planning their future and getting to know each other better...in every sense of the word.

"I'll get it," Harrison said, rising quickly from the living room sofa as Paige started to reach for her purse and the remainder of the five hundred dollars Bobby had given her. "Save some of that money for the baby's college fund."

What baby? Paige thought dazedly. Then she realized Harrison was talking about their child—the one they were going to have someday. Her heart warmed at the thought.

Harrison opened the front door, and there was a long silence. It was the pizza man, wasn't it? Paige thought. Then, to her horror, she heard her mother's voice.

"Harrison! My, I didn't expect to find you here."

Paige jumped up and joined Harrison at the door, acutely aware of the fact that she was in her robe at five-thirty in the afternoon. Thank goodness at least Harrison was decently dressed. Most of the weekend he'd been running around her apartment in gym shorts and little else.

"Hi, Mother!" Paige said with a forced cheerfulness. "What are you doing in Miami? Why didn't you call first? How was the rest of the cruise? Was the captain nice to you?"

Aurora hugged Paige. "One question at a time, darling. And then I get to ask a few of my own." She looked pointedly at Harrison, who appeared slightly green. "May I come in?"

"Oh, uh, sure." Paige pulled the door open wider and Aurora breezed in.

"First, I'm in Miami because that's where the cruise ship docked. I didn't call first because I wanted to surprise you. The rest of the cruise was divine, Captain Barnes bent over backward to make sure I was happy. And finally, I have some wonderful news. I got married!" She held up her left hand to reveal a stunning diamond ring.

Paige's heart sank, but for Aurora's sake she put on a brave face. "That's . . . wonderful. I'm so . . . happy for you. Doc Waller?"

Aurora smiled enigmatically. "He's parking the car, and he'll be up here in a few minutes."

Paige panicked. "Then I've got to get dressed!" she said, making a beeline for the bedroom. She was leaving poor Harrison to explain his presence to Aurora, but that couldn't be helped. Paige couldn't very well meet her new stepfather in her bathrobe.

Harrison didn't know quite what to say to Aurora, his future mother-in-law. It was embarrassing enough to be found cozily ensconced in Paige's apartment. But given the circumstances, he had more than the usual amount of explaining to do.

Thankfully, Aurora eased over the awkward moment. "So, it looks as if you and Paige resolved your differences," she said as she sat down on the sofa and pulled a cigarette from her purse. She looked around for an ashtray, seemed to think better of lighting up, and put the cigarette back where it came from. "I wondered why I didn't see you on the ship. I thought you were hiding from me."

Harrison cleared his throat. "No, ma'am. I got off the ship at Grand Cayman. I had to get things straightened out with Paige. I care for your daughter a great deal."

"Ma'am? Egad, Harrison, you're making me feel like a grandmother. After all, we were almost . . . well, you did buy me flowers and chocolates at one time." She batted her eyelashes flirtatiously.

"Please, I'd like to forget all about that," he said. "You do understand... I mean, did anyone explain to you that I was working undercover?"

"You mean you didn't really find me attractive?" she asked, her face falling.

A hot denial was on the tip of his tongue when Aurora grinned, and he realized she was deliberately teasing him. "I think you're a lovely woman, Aurora," he said. "Can we please leave it at that?"

She laughed. "Yes, of course. I couldn't resist razzing you, though. A man who plays the field the way you did can't expect to get off scot-free, now, can he?"

"No, ma'am. Umm, I mean, no, Aurora."

"Of course, I did slap you. I'm sorry for that. I'm always trying to fight Paige's battles for her . . . when it appears she's perfectly capable of handling you herself."

Harrison wasn't sure how he felt about being "handled." Fortunately, a smart knock on the door put an end to the uncomfortable conversation. Paige hadn't reappeared, so Harrison answered it.

A tall, silver-haired man Harrison had never seen before was standing uncertainly in the hallway. Since he wasn't holding a pizza box, Harrison could only conclude that he was Aurora's new husband.

"These darned apartments all look alike," the man said. "This is Paige Stovall's place, right?"

"Yes, it is. And you're . . ."

The man smiled broadly, revealing two rows of straight, white teeth. "Bobby Stovall, Paige's father."

"Harrison Powell," Harrison said dazedly as Bobby pumped his hand a couple of times. Paige's father, here, now? He hoped Bobby wasn't the jealous type, because Aurora's new husband was due to show up any moment.

"Ah, the mysterious Harrison," Bobby said. "I'm much obliged to you, sir, for getting the message to me that my two best girls were in trouble."

"Since I was the one who helped get them into trouble, it seemed the right thing to do," Harrison said, feeling more ill at ease by the moment. How was he ever going to convince Paige's parents that he was good enough for their daughter, when he'd been partially responsible for her being arrested?

Aurora rose from the couch and walked over to kiss her ex-husband on the cheek. "Hello, darling. Any trouble finding a parking place?"

The realization hit Harrison like a ton of bricks. Bobby wasn't just Aurora's ex; he was also her new husband. Harrison was just about to comment on this startling news when Paige reappeared, looking a bit hastily put together in jeans and a ruffled white blouse that needed a pressing. Her hair looked as if she'd run a frenzied brush through it, the flyaway strands sticking to her cheek. She was still adorable.

"Daddy?" she said, skidding to a stop. "What are you doing here? I mean, of course I'm happy to see you, but this is a rather inopportune time. Uh, could you maybe come back in a few minutes? Mother's, uh, friend is...and you can see how embarrassing it would be..."

Bobby and Aurora, arm in arm, just watched and waited for Paige to wind down. They both were wearing silly grins—grins reserved for people in love. Harrison was sure he'd been wearing one just like it all weekend.

The true situation finally hit Paige. Her eyes lit up and her mouth dropped open. "You?" she sputtered. "You're Mother's new husband?"

"Captain Barnes married us at sea," Aurora said. "Isn't that romantic?"

"Your mother talked me into finishing out the cruise with her, after all," Bobby explained. "You know I can never say no to her when she gets an idea in her head."

"We were actually planning to wait," Aurora added. "I wanted to plan a big, lavish wedding, since I never had one of those. But we just got carried away. You know, the sea air and all."

Finally jarred out of her stupor, Paige rushed over to hug them both. "I'm so happy for you! You have no idea how long I've been waiting for this moment. And, Mother, as for that big, lavish wedding you wanted—" she paused, slipped her arm around Harrison and sprang her own news "—how would you feel about planning one for your daughter instead?"

Harrison waited nervously for his future in-laws' reactions.

Bobby and Aurora stared at Paige, then looked at each other. Smiles slowly spread across their faces, and then they did something that baffled Harrison, something that seemed totally out of character. They gave each other a "high five."

"See, I told you it would work," Aurora said.

"I guess there is something to the benefits of sea air," Bobby agreed.

Paige put her hands on her hips. "What are you talking about?" she asked. Harrison was more than a little curious himself.

The pizza delivery man chose that moment to arrive. Harrison paid him and, not knowing what else to do, set the box on the coffee table in the living room. "Anyone for pizza?"

The other three people in the room didn't move. They simply stared at each other.

"Well, honey," Bobby finally said, "now that it's all ended happily, I suppose we should confess. Your mother and I reconciled before you took the cruise. But we were worried about you. You never seemed to meet any nice men, much less date them. So we, uh, came up with this story about needing you to go on the cruise with Aurora to protect her from getting hooked up with the wrong man. But really, all we wanted was for you to meet some fellas. And I guess it worked.''

Harrison held his breath. Paige looked ready to explode. ''You mean,'' she said, addressing her mother, ''that it was all an act? All the flirting and dancing? The late nights and the way you hung out with Doc Waller—it was all an act so I would follow you around and meet potential husbands?''

Aurora spread her hands helplessly. ''Well . . .''

Harrison caught Paige's eye. ''Hey, Paige, it did work. Can't argue with that.''

All at once the fight went out of Paige. She smiled tentatively, then chuckled, then laughed outright. ''If you two—no, you three,'' she said, including Harrison, ''aren't the worst bunch of schemers and manipulators I've ever met, I'll...I'll go on another cruise.''

''Sounds like she's serious,'' Bobby said. ''How about we eat this pizza before it gets cold?''

They all sat on the floor around the coffee table, even Aurora, and devoured the pizza. They washed it down with the last of a bottle of champagne Harrison and Paige had bought to celebrate their engagement.

Quarrels were forgotten as they talked about weddings and children and grandchildren. After a while Harrison sat back and listened to the lighthearted banter, thinking what a great family he was marrying into.

He pulled Paige against him, and she rested her head on his shoulder. He'd never seen her quite so relaxed, so happy. He'd like to take credit for her mood, but he knew her euphoria was at least partly due to her parents' reconciliation. They couldn't have given Paige a greater gift.

As for his own mood, he honestly couldn't remember when he'd felt this content, this complete. He would never again question his judgment when it came to women. He would never need to. The best one in the world had stolen his heart, and he intended to let her keep it.

* * * * *

SILHOUETTE Desire

COMING NEXT MONTH

ALEX AND THE ANGEL Dixie Browning

Man of the Month & Tall, Dark and Handsome

Alex Hightower had three women on his mind—his daughter, his girlfriend and Angeline Perkins. Angel was exciting and his daughter adored her, but surely she was not a likely marriage candidate?

WHEN SHE WAS BAD Ryanne Corey

Jenny had been good and pure all her life. Now she was going to be wild. Picking up Tray Malone was Jenny's first daring act, and she might already have bitten off more than she could chew!

THE SAINT OF BOURBON STREET BJ James

Men of the Black Watch

Katherine Rivard needed the help of a dangerous man to find her sister in the sewers of New Orleans and Mitch Ryan was a *very* dangerous man.

ALMOST A HONEYMOON Susan Crosby

Abducted by a leather-clad stranger who turned out to be her bodyguard, Paige O'Halloran wondered why he was hiding them away in a *honeymoon* cottage?

TWO-FACED WOMAN Lucy Gordon

A woman like private eye Debbie Harker could make a man's life heaven or hell. Hell cop Jake Garfield knew about. But not heaven—at least not yet…

THE MAN FROM ATLANTIS Judith McWilliams

Jenna Faron stumbled across a gorgeous male in the desert, and didn't want to let him go seeing as attractive, single men weren't exactly coming out of the woodwork. However, he was a *little* unusual…

Southern Knights

by

Marilyn Pappano

A police detective. An FBI agent. A government prosecutor. Three men for whom friendship and the law mean everything. Three men for whom true love has remained elusive—until now.

Join award-winning author Marilyn Pappano as she brings her **Southern Knights** mini-series to Sensation, starting in February with MICHAEL'S GIFT.

> Michael Bennett didn't know why Valery Navarre had come to him when she was in peril. He was a total stranger to her. Yet he couldn't refuse to help her, not after her image had been branded on his mind—and his heart.

And look out for the other two **Southern Knights**:

March 1996
REGARDING REMY

April 1996
A MAN LIKE SMITH

▼ SILHOUETTE

Sensation

Fl wer P wer

How would you like to win a year's supply of sophisticated and deeply emotional romances? Well, you can and they're free! Simply unscramble the words below and send the completed puzzle to us by 31st July 1996. The first 5 correct entries picked after the closing date will win a years supply of Silhouette Special Edition novels (six books every month—worth over £150).

1	LTIUP	TULIP
2	FIDLADFO	DAFFODIL
3	ERSO	ROSE
4	AHTNYHCI	HYACINTH
5	GIBANOE	
6	NEAPUTI	PETUNIA
7	YDSIA	DAISY
8	SIIR	IRIS
9	NNAIATCRO	
10	LDIAAH	DAHLIA
11	RRSEOIMP	PRIMROSE
12	LEGXFOOV	FOXGLOVE
13	OYPPP	POPPY
14	LZEAAA	AZALEA
15	COIRDH	ORCHID

Please turn over for details of how to enter ☞

Hw t enter

Listed overleaf are 15 jumbled-up names of flowers. All you have to do is unscramble the names and write your answer in the space provided. We've done the first one for you!

When you have found all the words, don't forget to fill in your name and address in the space provided below and pop this page into an envelope (you don't need a stamp) and post it today. Hurry—competition ends 31st July 1996.

Silhouette Flower Puzzle
FREEPOST
Croydon
Surrey
CR9 3WZ

Are you a Reader Service Subscriber?   Yes ☐   No ☐

Ms/Mrs/Miss/Mr _____

Address _____

_____

_____ Postcode _____

One application per household.

COMP196
A